BOOK EXCHANGE

W9-BJD-060

(803) 760-6647

Jan's heart thumped erratically in her chest. She'd recognize that lithe form anywhere.

"This is private property," he said.

Jan discovered that she disliked him in equal measure to her unbidden, reluctant attraction to him. "*My* private property," she told him, not without relish.

"I see. I assume you plan to sell it.... If you do, I'd like first refusal."

It didn't seem too much to give him, but something held her back.

He said, "Where do you plan to stay the night?"

"Here."

There was a glint of irritation in the frigid depths of his eyes. "Do you know how to work the range? The water?"

Tilting her chin, she said, "I'll be perfectly all right."

And she enjoyed a fierce satisfaction when his mouth curved into a slow smile that was both sinister and sexy as hell.

"Don't play games with me," he said softly.

BOOK EXCHANGE
3101 ASHLEY PHOSPHATE RD., #11
NORTH CHARLESTON, SC 29418
(803) 552-0037

INTRODUCTION TO SERIES

Olivia Nicholls and the two half sisters Anet and
Jan Carruthers are all born survivors—but, so far,
unlucky in love. Things change, however, when an
eighteenth-century miniature portrait of a beautiful
and mysterious young woman passes into each of their
hands. It may be coincidence, it may not! The portrait
is meant to be a charm to bring love to the lives of
those who possess it—but there is one condition:

I found Love as you'll find yours,
and trust it will be true,
This Portrait is a fated charm
To speed your Love to you.

But if you be not Fortune's Fool
Once your heart's Desire is nigh,
Pass on my likeness as Cupid's Tool
Or your Love will fade and die.

The Final Proposal is Jan's story and the concluding
title in Robyn Donald's captivating new trilogy
THE MARRIAGE MAKER.

Don't miss any of our special offers. Write to us at the
following address for information on our newest releases.

Harlequin Reader Service
U.S.: 3010 Walden Ave., P.O. Box 1325, Buffalo, NY 14269
Canadian: P.O. Box 609, Fort Erie, Ont. L2A 5X3

ROBYN DONALD

The Final Proposal

Harlequin Books

TORONTO • NEW YORK • LONDON
AMSTERDAM • PARIS • SYDNEY • HAMBURG
STOCKHOLM • ATHENS • TOKYO • MILAN
MADRID • WARSAW • BUDAPEST • AUCKLAND

If you purchased this book without a cover you should be aware
that this book is stolen property. It was reported as "unsold and
destroyed" to the publisher, and neither the author nor the
publisher has received any payment for this "stripped book."

ISBN 0-373-11877-5

THE FINAL PROPOSAL

First North American Publication 1997.

Copyright © 1996 by Robyn Donald.

All rights reserved. Except for use in any review, the reproduction or
utilization of this work in whole or in part in any form by any electronic,
mechanical or other means, now known or hereafter invented, including
xerography, photocopying and recording, or in any information storage
or retrieval system, is forbidden without the written permission of the
publisher, Harlequin Enterprises Limited, 225 Duncan Mill Road,
Don Mills, Ontario, Canada M3B 3K9.

All characters in this book have no existence outside the imagination of
the author and have no relation whatsoever to anyone bearing the same
name or names. They are not even distantly inspired by any individual
known or unknown to the author, and all incidents are pure invention.

This edition published by arrangement with Harlequin Books S.A.

® and TM are trademarks of the publisher. Trademarks indicated with
® are registered in the United States Patent and Trademark Office, the
Canadian Trade Marks Office and in other countries.

Printed in U.S.A.

CHAPTER ONE

'GERRY, I look completely ridiculous. Nobody in their right mind wears clothes like this to a celebrity polo tournament!' Jan Carruthers stared at her reflection with appalled fascination as her cousin carefully settled a wide-brimmed hat onto her short, auburn hair. Some milliner, crazed by romanticism, had draped both crown and brim with what looked to be the entire stock of a florist's shop.

'That,' Gerry said smugly, stepping back to gaze at her, 'is the whole idea. When you do "before and after" shots, you always make the "before" shot as outrageous as you can. You, little coz, are now definitely, extravagantly, magnificently conspicuous—just the way you should look.'

'I should have told you to find some other midget when you came up with this absurd scheme.'

'You did, several times. But I'm cunning, and I know all your weak spots. As soon as I mentioned all those poor women who think it's necessary to spend thousands of dollars to look good, you wavered. Then I pointed out that you could donate the money you're going to earn to your centre for troubled girls. Being the noble-minded sucker that you are, you couldn't say no.'

'It's not *my* centre, and I'd have turned you down without a moment's thought if I'd known you were going to dress me up as a mushroom.' Jan glowered down at the narrow-skirted silk suit in palest peach. Worn to a fashionable lunch it would have been perfect; it would be totally out of place at the polo ground just south of Auckland.

'No, you wouldn't have.' Secure in her model's figure, and with her extra eight inches of height, Gerry radiated satisfaction. 'Stop grumbling—of course you look like a mushroom. Women who are only five foot two can't wear hats like cartwheels. Just be grateful we didn't decide on the toadstool look, and make the hat scarlet with big white spots.'

The far too many people needed to set up a photographic shoot for a fashion magazine sniggered. Clearly this rare opportunity to indulge themselves with flagrantly bad taste was giving them all a sneaky forbidden pleasure.

'Besides,' Gerry pointed out mercilessly, 'your centre for disturbed girls needs all the money it can get. Didn't I see in the newspaper that the government has just cut the grant by fifty per cent?'

'And fifty per cent of a shoestring is a thread,' Jan muttered, still feeling the sick dismay the news had caused.

Gerry surveyed her with affectionate resignation. 'Under that glossily smart, sophisticated, hip exterior you're the most motherly creature I've ever come across. Why don't you get married and have kids of your own instead of spending most of your spare time worrying about, raising money for and counselling your wayward girls?'

'They are not *my* girls, and they are not all wayward!'

'Oh, semantics! In need of care and attention, then— and don't you dare frown!'

Jan froze. It had taken so long for her make-up to be applied that she didn't dare risk cracking it. More for form's sake than from conviction, she said, 'I warn you, I'll have strong hysterics if anyone so much as smirks.'

The hairdresser, a nervy young man with a shaven head set off by a diamond stud in his ear, said fretfully, 'I still think she should be wearing a wig. With ringlets.'

'No,' Jan said, as forcefully as she could through stiff lips.

Gerry sighed. 'She's right. We don't want to slide over the edge into farce. She has to look as though some poor woman could make the same mistakes.'

'A madwoman.' Jan leaned forward to peer at the coating of blue mascara on her black lashes. Flinching, she closed her eyes and backed away from the mirror. 'I must be crazy! I'm an image consultant—I show people what their most flattering colours and styles are, I teach them how to wear clothes so they look great and I'm moderately famous for my seminars and workshops on self-esteem—I don't prance through magazine pages as a glaring example of what *not* to do.' Ignoring Gerry's outcry she chewed her lip, carefully and sultrily coloured a shade that clashed subtly with the suit *and* her ivory skin.

'The "after" pages will reveal you as your true, impeccably elegant self,' Gerry reminded her with cheerful callousness. 'Come on, let Cindy redo your mouth and then put this bracelet on.'

'Diamonds!' Recoiling, Jan almost lost her balance as the ankle-wrecking high heels on her Italian shoes sank into the grass. 'Oh, damn these things! They're going to kill me before this is over. Gerry, you'll never get away with this. Talk about a Victorian nightmare!'

'We don't *want* to get away with anything,' Gerry said, casting her eyes heavenward. 'The bracelet is absolutely perfect.'

'I might lose it. Though I'd be doing the world a favour if I did. Or it might be stolen,' Jan muttered through set lips while the make-up woman reapplied lipstick.

'You're too conscientious and sensible to lose anything, and although I know New Zealand seems to be trying to catch up with the rest of the world as far as crime rates go, there's not likely to be a master jewel thief at a polo match. Anyway, we've got a security man. And that bracelet is just the right overdone touch. So shut up and hold your arm out. Think of what you can do with the money at your half-a-shoestring centre.'

It was the only redeeming feature of this whole episode. Closing her eyes again, Jan schooled her features into long-suffering patience and submitted to being fettered by the heavy, ostentatious snake of diamonds and gold.

'Great,' Gerry said, gloating. 'You look awful. Actually, damn you, you don't—in spite of our best efforts you just about manage to get away with it. Shows what little chicken bones and huge, dark blue eyes set on an exotic slant will do for a woman. To say nothing of that sensual pout. Just think, snooks, if you'd been ten inches taller you'd be a millionaire model.'

Jan snorted. 'I haven't the stamina for it. Anyway, I'd be be over the hill by now.'

'But *rich*, love, filthy rich—because the camera adores you. And nowadays quite a few models last beyond their thirty-first birthday. You'd be one—there isn't a wrinkle on that fabulous skin.'

'Everyone's got wrinkles,' Jan said morosely. 'And I'm not thirty-one until tomorrow.'

'Ha—more semantics! I'm really looking forward to tonight—you and Aunt Cynthia know how to make a birthday party hum. But first we have to get this over with. OK, let's go out there—and don't forget to simper for the camera.'

Jan batted her lashes dramatically. 'You'll never see a more perfect simper. Damn, I can barely move in these shoes. I need crutches. Or a large, oiled Nubian slave to carry me around.'

Unimpressed, Gerry grinned. 'Sorry, slaves are off today. Anyway, an oiled one would mark the suit. You'll cope. You've got that inborn aplomb that makes the rest of us feel inferior. And remember, it's for a good cause. There are hundreds of thousands of women in New Zealand and Australia who are dying to discover that they can go anywhere, any time, with a good, basic wardrobe that isn't going to cost them a fortune.'

'I still think just showing the right gear would have been enough.'

'It lacks drama. Trust me. Besides, this is good publicity for you.'

'Good publicity?' Jan almost choked. 'I'll probably never see another client.'

'Rubbish! Everyone will look at the "after" shots and understand what we've done.'

'And if you believe that,' Jan said sweetly, picking her way out of the tent and into the blinding sunlight of a late New Zealand summer, 'I have the latitude and longitude of a shipwreck off Fiji and I know for a fact that all the gold is still on board. I'll sell you the treasure map for a million dollars.'

Outside, champagne glass in hand, she posed for the camera, keeping her gaze fixed and slightly unfocused, because most of the spectators at the celebrity tournament found the sight of an overdressed woman being photographed every bit as fascinating as the game. People she knew grinned, waved and settled back to stare quite unashamedly, but even complete strangers seemed to feel that the camera gave them licence to watch.

Jan was accustomed to being looked at; it was, to some extent, part of her job. At seminars and workshops she frequently stood in front of large audiences and, without anything more than a few minor bubbles in her stomach, kept them interested.

This, however, was different. She felt as though she'd been dumped into the modern equivalent of medieval stocks.

It didn't help when the photographer, damn him, entered wholeheartedly into the theatrical ambience of the occasion and began giving a running commentary.

'Everyone's an actor,' Jan hissed after he'd told her to shake her sexy little hips. 'Shut up!'

'But this is how photographers are supposed to behave,' he said, narrowing his eyes lustfully at her. 'You've seen the films and read the books. Come on, darling, give me a slow, come-hither grin—make like a volcano...'

Resisting the impulse to stick out her tongue, she tossed her head, catching as she did so the eyes of a man a few feet away. Until then he'd been intent upon the game, but apparently Sid's babble had intruded on his concentration. Dark brows compressed, he scrutinised them.

Growing up with a tall, big-framed stepfather and a half-sister who took after him should have taught Jan not to be intimidated by mere stature, but Anet and Stephen Carruthers were gentle people. Once she'd discovered that some men used their height and build to intimidate, Jan had rapidly developed a small woman's wariness.

And the stranger *was* tall, with broad shoulders and heavily muscled legs and thighs beneath skin-tight jodhpurs.

Something about him—possibly his relaxed stance, the almost feline grace that held the promise of instant, decisive response—tested the barriers she'd erected over the years.

Trying to reinforce them, she gave him her most aloofly objective gaze and decided that he'd photograph well. Angular bone structure gave strength and a certain striking severity to his features, a hard edge intensified by straight browns and a wide, imperiously moulded mouth. His bronzed, bone-deep tan indicated a life spent outside, as did the long, corded muscles in his arms. And he had a good head of hair, wavy and conventionally cut by an expert, the glossy brown heated by the sun to a rich mahogany.

He had to be a professional polo player, in New Zealand for the celebrity tournament. Perhaps he was playing in the next game.

Beside him stood a girl even taller than Gerry, a girl, Jan noticed automatically, dressed with exactly the right note of casual elegance. As Jan watched she said something, her stance revealing a certain tentativeness. Instantly he switched that intent, oddly remote gaze from Jan to the girl, and answered. His companion blushed, her carefully cultivated poise vanishing like mist in the fierce light of the sun. His smile was a masterpiece, the sort that seduced women without even trying—indolent, confident and compelling.

And you'd better get a hold of yourself, Jan commanded herself sternly. You're here to do a job, not drool over some wandering sportsman, even if he does have more magnetism in one black eyebrow than most other men have in their whole bodies.

Eventually, thank heavens, Gerry said, 'OK, that should do it. Let's get back into the tent and change into the "after" gear.'

'Just a couple more,' Sid decided. 'Jan, stand by the hoardings, will you? I want to get a horse or two in the background.'

Jan cast a swift glance at the field. Most of the game was taking place in the middle of the paddock, well away from the advertisements that separated the playing ground from the spectators, so she'd be safe enough.

Moving as gracefully as she could in the ridiculous heels, she walked across, obeying Sid's request to watch the horses.

'That's good,' he said. 'Try a smile. OK—a sort of faint, yearning one, as though your lover's out there and you're going to see him again tonight.'

What lover? Jan thought sardonically. Still, she did her best, keeping the smile pinned in place even when horses and riders suddenly changed direction and thundered towards her. She stepped back at the moment a breeze whipped the ludicrous hat off her head and sent it cartwheeling out into the paddock, straight into the path of one of the horses.

Rigid, Jan watched as the horse reared and tripped, sending its rider to one side as it came down and slid towards her, a huge, squealing mass of gleaming chestnut.

Even as she tottered backward Jan knew she was doomed. Faintly, she was aware of yells. A woman screamed.

Suddenly she was grasped by steel-strong hands and hauled back and to one side, snatched by the sheer force of her rescuer's momentum into safety. At the same time the horse splintered through the hoardings, then amazingly got to its feet, sweating, shaking its head as its eyes rolled.

Jan was thrust aside and her rescuer, the man with the deadly smile, moved with slow, steady steps towards the trembling horse, talking to it in a voice that was deep and lazy and gentle. Jan couldn't hear what he was saying above the hammer of her heart, but like everyone else she watched, spellbound.

'Are you all right?' Gerry whispered, grabbing her.

Jan nodded, pulling away from her cousin's hold and clenching her teeth to hold back the shivers that had come abruptly out of nowhere.

A lean, tanned hand caught the horse's bridle and held it firmly while the other hand stroked up the dripping neck. The man's voice, textured with a magic as primal and compelling as the partnership between man and beast, crooned the nervous, panting horse into quiescence while the rider, fortunately unhurt by his tumble, approached.

Time got going again. Jan's rescuer said something to the polo player that made him laugh, and then relinquished his charge and turned back, heading straight for Jan.

'Are you all right?' he demanded.

The same words Gerry had used, but where her tone had been anxious his was accusing.

Although that swift, hard embrace had wrenched every bone in her body, Jan said, 'I'm fine. Is the horse?'

He had amazing eyes, smouldering silver between thick, curly lashes, and he was in a towering rage. 'If it is, it's no thanks to you,' he said, his voice curt as a whiplash. 'Horses are not props, and that damned hat of yours could have killed both the rider and the horse, as well as you.'

Jan nodded. Her eyes felt huge in her face and she was dry-mouthed, unable to think let alone speak.

'Get her something to drink,' he ordered Gerry, without any softening in his manner. 'Tea, not alcohol, and put plenty of sugar in it.'

Astonishingly Gerry—capable, sensible Gerry—said meekly, 'Yes, all right,' and turned away.

'I'll go with you,' Jan croaked.

But her knees shook. When she tried to walk they gave way and she stumbled. To her utter mortification her rescuer picked her up with casual, insulting ease and carried her into the tent, away from the horses and the sun and the whispering crowd.

Her nostrils quivered, sensitised to a particular scent, faint, masculine, so potent that she could feel its effects in every cell in her body. Abnormally conscious of the smooth, coiled power in her rescuer's strong arms and shoulders, Jan raised her lashes and saw in his bronzed throat the steady pulsing of his heartbeat.

For some reason her eyes filled with tears. Blinking fiercely, she dragged her gaze away and stared straight ahead, more shocked by the exaggerated response of her body than by the danger she had just escaped. Being aware of a man was one thing; this, she thought feverishly, was another and entirely more hazardous reaction. He overloaded her senses.

Inside the tent, he set her on her feet, and the heat of his body was replaced by a chill that struck through to her bones. Shivering, she collapsed into a folding chair that someone pushed towards her, kicking her shoes off. The man who had saved her life looked at her feet, brows climbing.

'They scarcely look big enough to support an adult,' he said.

It was not a compliment, but Jan's bones liquefied.

'We're so very grateful for your quick thinking,' Gerry said, turning her famous, slow smile onto the man.

He responded with a remark and an ironic, knowledgeable smile of his own. A visibly affected Gerry accompanied him from the tent.

'God,' the hairdresser said beneath his breath as he handed Jan a mug of tea, 'I wish I had half his pulling power!'

Jan cupped her hands around the mug, waiting for them to stop trembling. Hearing without understanding the chatter of the crew about her, she sipped the hot liquid, taking exaggerated care not to spill it. She felt bruised and battered, her bones aching. Tomorrow, she thought grimly, she'd have fingermarks imprinted on her skin. Still, if he hadn't acted with the speed and brute force of a hunting animal she could well have ended up under the horse, and then bruises would have been the least of her worries.

'How do you feel?' Gerry asked, approaching her with a frown that didn't hide the anxiety in her expression.

Jan put the half-empty mug down and got to her feet, wavering slightly but determined. 'I feel a bit shaky,' she said, 'but I'll be fine. Hadn't we better get the rest of the shots done?'

'Are you sure you can manage it?'

'Positive,' Jan said. 'Help me off with this wretched suit, will you?'

It took all of her self-assurance to walk again through the entrance of the tent and into the sun. Even though she'd expected the sudden shift of attention, she was embarrassed by it.

At least the 'after' gear suited the occasion perfectly—a honey-coloured shirt and matching skirt in fine cotton. Beneath the shirt was a silk singlet a shade lighter, and instead of the Italian shoes she wore low heels, perfect for picking her way across the grass. The diamond horror was replaced by a thin gold chain wound several times around her small wrist, and she carried a sleek, unadorned parasol.

This time Sid was his normal silent self, and the shoot finished quickly. Posing, looking wistful, smiling, Jan wanted nothing more than to be out of this and safely at home—away from all the eyes, away from the man who had looked at her with such charged antipathy.

Thank heavens he was nowhere in sight.

And she was there as a model, not to search the polo field for a stranger. So she kept her eyes resolutely away from the game and her mind on what she was doing.

However, just before she slipped back into the tent she saw him on a black horse. A primitive, unexpected alertness stirred her senses as she watched the rider reach over and hit the ball, then, with a skilled hand on the reins, gather his steed for a rapid change of direction.

'Who are you looking at?' Gerry asked. 'Oh, him—he's gorgeous, isn't he?' She grinned. 'Definitely hero material, even though he made me feel like a worm. Too big for you, though—we all know you like smaller men.'

'I don't mind big men provided they don't tread on me,' Jan said, switching her gaze to a friend who was waving from further along the field. Waving back, she said, 'I grew up with a big man—and a big sister.'

'How is Anet? And that utterly glamorous hunk of a husband of hers?'

'Still besotted with each other. They're checking out some lost plateau in Venezuela at the moment.'

'They can have that. Too hot by far for me.' Gerry blew a curl back from her face. 'In fact, *this* is too hot for me. Do you want to stay and watch?'

'No, thanks. I don't know the rules.'

'What you really mean is that country pursuits bore you,' Gerry accused.

'Well, I'm a city woman at heart.' Jan smiled at a woman she'd served on a committee with. 'Hello, Sue.'

Sue gushed, 'I nearly *died* when I saw that horse slide onto you! Trust you to be rescued by some god-like being! You didn't get hurt at all? And who was he?'

Once Jan had assured her that yes, she'd been scooped clean out of the horse's way, and no, she didn't know her rescuer's name, Sue urged, 'Join us, both of you.'

'I'd love to,' Jan said, 'but I can't, I'm sorry.'

It wasn't the only invitation they turned down. All of Auckland, it seemed, was at the polo tournament, and determined to enjoy it.

As they threaded their way through the crowd Gerry looked around. 'Between us,' she said, 'we probably know everyone here.'

'If you go back far enough in the family tree we're probably related to most of them,' Jan said. 'New Zealand's pretty small.'

'Do you ever want to go and find a bigger pool to swim in?'

Jan shook her head. 'I thoroughly enjoyed the three years I spent overseas, but this is home.'

'I know how you feel,' Gerry said peacefully. 'Little it might be, but there's something about the place.'

The sun was only half way to the horizon when Jan drove her small, elderly, much cosseted MG into the garage of her townhouse in Mount Eden, one of three in a new block hidden from the street by a high, lime-washed wall. Once inside, she stripped off her shoes and, wiggling her toes on the cool, smooth tiles, rang her mother.

'Hello, darling,' Cynthia said enthusiastically. 'How did the photo shoot go?'

'Well...' Because she'd soon hear it from someone, Jan told her about the incident, soothing her natural maternal alarm by assuring her that she was completely unhurt.

'At the *polo*,' Cynthia lamented, as though somehow it was especially outrageous that such a thing should have happened there.

'Ah, well, I was rescued by a superb man,' Jan said. 'I wish I could thank him!'

Jan recalled the splintering anger in those frigid eyes and shivered. 'I'm not likely to see him again,' she said, and changed the subject. 'I thought I'd have a shower and then come on over.'

'Oh, no, you don't,' her mother said sternly. 'You'll arrive at exactly eight o'clock. Everything is under control. The caterers are doing all the hard work. The flowers are done. The house is spotless. I don't need you dashing around getting in the way, so have a rest. Make a cup of tea. Wallow in the bath. Read a book. Don't come near this place until we're all ready for you!'

Laughing, Jan gave in. Her mother much preferred to prepare for her parties in her own way.

She put the receiver down and wandered out onto the terrace. Ahead, in blissful solitude, stretched the afternoon and early evening. The polo stunt had been the last of the photographic shoots, for which Jan was extremely thankful. In a couple of months Gerry's article and the photos would appear in the magazine.

Her cousin had even promised to slip in a mention of the centre, and that group of dedicated, mostly unpaid women who worked with and worried about the girls and young women brought to them—many in severe trouble, most just trembling on the brink of it.

Money, Jan thought; it all came down to money. Or the lack of it.

A van, which would be enormously useful, was just a pipedream.

Still, she thought drily as she moved a lounger into the shade of the sky-flower vine that rambled over her pergola, Gerry's project would put some extra money in the coffers.

*　　*　　*

She must have gone to sleep, because although the telephone bell invaded her dreams like a berserk bee she was unable to wake herself up in time to answer it. Whoever it was hadn't left a message, so it wasn't a summons from the centre. However, the imperative call had destroyed her serenity, leaving her to wander restlessly around the house looking for something to do.

Yawning, she wondered how the trip was going. Ten of the girls who'd been recommended to the centre by a social agency were with selected adults at a camp on one of the islands in the Hauraki Gulf. A weekend wasn't long enough, of course, but it would help.

Unfortunately, they needed more than an occasional weekend if the lessons they learned there about their capabilities, and the self-esteem they gained, were to stick with them. On the centre's wish-list was a camp of their own, where the girls could stay for several weeks if needed, away from the many temptations of the city and from bad companions.

Another pipedream.

A few weeks ago Jan and her committee had worked out how much they needed. 'We're not asking for a lot— just the world,' one of the women had said, staring glumly at the figures.

Now, as she recalled the enormous set-up costs, Jan's heart quailed. Over the last few years she'd organised exhaustive and very vigorous fundraising to build up their financial base. They no longer had to worry about the rent, and they could afford the social worker's salary, but, as costs climbed and more girls turned up on their doorstep, they needed another paid social worker.

Every year they still had to go cap-in-hand to various organisations just to get money to struggle along.

So many organisations, all worthwhile, all seeking a share from the public's generosity.

'I must be running out of steam,' she told the potted bay tree out on the terrace as she watered it.

Thirty-one was not old, but it did seem to mark some sort of milestone. Perhaps it was the siren call of her hormones, warning her that time was frittering away.

For the first time Jan didn't want the party her mother planned with such care to mark each birthday. It was a family tradition, the end-of-summer, welcome-to-autumn party, and friends and relatives from all over the city and its environs came to wish her luck and enjoy themselves enormously.

Possibly this feeling of slow melancholy was what another of her cousins had warned her about.

'It's a crunch year—everyone has one,' she'd said, smiling wryly. 'Mine was my thirtieth. I woke up in tears, and wept all day. Everyone thought I was mad, but it's surprising how many women have one awful birthday— usually in their early thirties.'

Jan had enjoyed her thirtieth, which made it ridiculous to feel so ambivalent about her thirty-first. 'Stop right there,' she told herself aloud, wandering into the kitchen to pour herself a glass of feijoa and grapefruit juice.

Her gaze fell on the gaily wrapped present her half-sister had given her the day she and her husband left for their South American trip, with instructions to open it just before the party.

Where were they now, Anet and her husband of almost a year? Slashing their way through some tropical jungle, probably. For the first time, Jan allowed herself to admit that she envied Anet and Lucas the unmeasured, consuming love they shared.

Because she'd never fallen in love.

Not once.

Oh, there'd been a lover when she was twenty—she shivered, recalling the painful, humiliating end to that affair, if affair it could be called—and since then several men had asked her to marry them. A couple of them she'd liked and been attracted to, but she hadn't ever felt that complete confidence, the essential trust that allowed normally sensible and wary people to confide their life and their happiness to another person.

She just wanted everything, she thought sardonically: the electric, passionate involvement, the eager companionship and the complete faith in each other. And if she couldn't have it all, she wouldn't settle for less.

Relishing the tangy flavour of her drink, she sipped slowly while into her mind came an image of the man who had wrenched her out of the way of the horse.

A disturbing heat expanded through her. He had presence. However, that wasn't why she remembered him. She was accustomed to men with presence; her stepfather had it, so did Lucas. And so did Drake Arundell, the husband of a great friend of hers.

The stranger had more than presence; he possessed a disciplined, formidable authority that sent out warning signals. And he moved with the dangerous, predatory swiftness of a hunter.

Finishing the juice, she eyed the dishwasher, then with a half-laugh washed the glass and put it away.

'He's probably just your ordinary, average polo player,' she said firmly as she walked across the passage to her office. 'Overpaid, oversexed and over here.'

Weaving fantasies about a man she didn't know and wasn't likely to see again was stupid and futile. Life was not slipping by; she helped people as best she could, she was good at what she did and she earned good money doing it—and she had a warm, appreciative family. If she never married she'd be a superb aunt to Anet and Lucas's children when they had some.

Perhaps she should see about getting a cat.

Dressed in a smooth-fitting ivory dress, its neat lines conforming discreetly to her body, Jan walked with her mother across the big sitting room and out onto the wide terrace. A group of her friends were already there, and as she came through the French windows they began clapping, and called out birthday wishes.

'You look great,' Gerry said exuberantly when they had a moment to talk. She, as befitted an entirely more dramatic personality, wore a floating outfit of purples and blues and plum.

'Thanks,' Jan said lightly.

Gerry eyed the demure dress. 'You're well covered up. Bruises?'

'A few,' Jan admitted. 'Nothing to worry about.'

'I should have anchored that damned hat,' Gerry sighed.

'Yes, well, I'm just glad that no one got hurt. And that the horse and the rider were OK.'

'The hero was gorgeous,' her cousin said thoughtfully. 'I wonder who he was.'

'One of the polo players.'

'Perhaps we should have suggested your mother invite a few.' She leered unconvincingly. 'They'd give your party a certain *je ne sais quoi*. All those splendid muscles rippling beneath their shirts. Not to forget the equally splendid ones beneath—' Stopped by Jan's raised brows, she broke into a gurgle of laughter and finished, 'In their legs.'

'Most of them probably can't string more than ten words together,' Jan said, knowing she was being unfair.

'Who cares? They look like gods.'

'Centaurs.'

Gerry laughed. 'OK, although they're not exactly joined at the waist to their horses. And even if they can't speak in words of more than two syllables, we could just sip a little champagne and admire their form. Speaking of which— Oh, good Lord—'

Jan turned to follow her entranced gaze. There, standing beside Sally Porter, a friend from schooldays, and directing that killer smile at her mother, stood the man who had saved Jan from being squashed a few hours ago—all six feet two or three of him.

'Sally's latest?' Gerry muttered. 'I didn't see her at the polo, but of course she could have been there.'

Jan barely heard her. A hateful, febrile anticipation prickled through her.

'I'd better go and greet them,' she said with enormous reluctance when she saw her mother look across to her.

'I'll come with you,' Gerry offered, trying to sound heroic.

Together, they threaded their way across the terrace and inside. Sally, redheaded and vivacious, waved cheerfully. Not a muscle moving in his face, the man beside her watched them walk across the room.

'Darling,' Cynthia said warmly, 'I forgot to tell you that Sally was bringing her cousin with her.'

His name was Kear Lannion, and for some reason the fact that he was Sally's cousin was important.

Jan's wary gaze met pale, crystalline eyes and a cool, unsettling smile. Suddenly, violently, awakened to awareness, she rescued her own smile from the oblivion to which shock had consigned it. 'But we've met,' she said woodenly, holding out her hand. To her mother she explained, 'Kear was the man who probably saved my life this afternoon.'

He took her hand gently, tempering his strength to her slender bones. 'Jan,' he said, in a voice that was deep and rough enough to send a sensual shiver down her spine. 'It suits you.'

Pierced by swift, sharp antagonism, she smiled. 'Short and snappy?'

His glance mocked her. 'Well, no, that's not exactly what I had in mind. Have you fully recovered?'

'Yes, thank you.'

She wasn't going to mention her bruises. Neither, although she had to bite back the words, was she going to explain what she'd been doing in that stupid outfit. And she was not going to tell him that he'd only seen the 'before' picture. Especially not that, because if she did he'd realise she'd noticed his absence during the 'after' session.

But oh, how she wanted to! She even found herself hoping that Gerry would make the explanations. Unfortunately, smiling and fluttering her lashes in a manner Jan found vaguely annoying, Gerry confined her conversation to social pleasantries.

Her mother thanked him fervently, ending with, 'What a coincidence that you should be Sally's cousin.'

'The handsomest of my cousins,' Sally informed them with relish. If she'd hoped to embarrass him she failed; he gave her that slow smile and, close relative though she was, she lost her place before summoning the poise to continue, 'The most athletic too. I think the New Zealand team is going to lose half its fans now that Kear's stopped playing.'

Interestedly, Gerry said, 'Oh, have you retired?'

'I can't give it the time I need to pull my weight. So, yes, today was my last game for New Zealand.'

Another group of people came in through the door. By the time Jan had done her duty by them and found someone for them to talk to, Sally and Kear were deep in discussion with Gerry and another woman on the terrace.

Jan kept well away, but an hour or so later his deep, distinctive voice said from behind her, 'You look as though you could do with a refill. What would you like?'

'Orange juice, but I can get it.'

'It's no trouble,' he said. Together they walked across to the temporary bar.

'Are you a teetotaller?' he asked when the barman had served her.

'No, but when you're my size half a glass is enough to make you uncomfortably hot,' she said, wondering why her skin felt too tight for her.

'Wise woman.'

Shrugging, she returned, 'One learns.' She covertly searched for someone she could leave him with in a little while, when it wouldn't be too obvious that she was running away.

Just as the silence between them began to stretch uncomfortably he commented, 'Did I bruise you when I hurled you out of the way?' His gaze rested a moment on the sleeves and neckline of her dress.

CHAPTER TWO

JAN'S skin warmed under that deliberate survey. Hoping he hadn't noticed her hesitation, she said, 'It's nothing. And I don't think I thanked you for saving me.'

'I'm sorry about the bruising,' he said. 'As for your thanks, you didn't get a chance. I was too busy berating you.'

Startled, she looked up into eyes that shimmered like moonlight on water, a surface silver and translucent yet impossible to see beneath.

'You had a point,' she said, wondering why her mouth was so dry. 'The hat should have been pinned on. Is the horse really all right?'

'Yes, apart from a few bruises.' He didn't attempt to hide the surprise in his tone.

Defensively, she said, 'I was worried about it. Life is bad enough for a polo pony without—'

His brows rose. 'Polo ponies are fed like kings and cared for with the utmost devotion. They seem to enjoy the whole experience.'

'I hope so.' It had sounded ungracious, so she added, 'Lots of people think animals are like machines—disposable.'

'I earn my living from animals. Only a fool doesn't care for them.'

Sally had told them he was a farmer. Before Jan could stop herself she said shortly, 'Exploiting them.'

'Perhaps. But as long as humans eat meat there'll be farmers. I make sure my animals are looked after and not treated cruelly, and that their death is quick and painless. Which is more than could be said for most animals in the wild.'

25

'At least in the wild they're free,' she said, more to provoke than because she believed what she was saying.

His smile was ironic. 'Freedom is a human concept. And, even for *Homo sapiens*, a full belly and security are more important than any illusory freedom.'

She said, 'Goodness, you're a cynic.'

'I'm a realist.' His tone was dry as Chardonnay. 'Most people who live in the country are. When your livelihood is at the mercy of the elements you very soon learn that nature doesn't value any one thing above the other. Humanity is no more important than animals, and no less.'

She said pertly, 'So rural life teaches one lessons. I must remember that next time I stay with friends in the country.'

'I gather you don't go often.'

'How did you guess?' She widened her eyes like those women who believed rapt, slightly glazed stares were a good substitute for conversation. 'I get twitchy if I'm too far from a bookshop or café. However, if the air didn't smell so peculiar I might be tempted to go more often.'

She'd caught his attention well and truly. 'The air?'

'Well, there's no body to it. It hardly seems natural, somehow.'

His mouth twitched. 'No exhaust fumes.'

He was watching her, not with the interest of a man for a woman he was attracted to, but measuringly, as though he'd like to know what made her tick. A nameless sensation clutched her stomach, tangling her thoughts into incoherence.

'Exactly,' she said, smiling, but thinking, I have to get away from here! Failing that, she needed a neutral subject; the usual rules didn't seem to apply to this man. Teasing him, however mildly, was too much like walking along the edge of a cliff. 'Sally said you live by the sea. In the Bay of Islands?'

'No, further north,' he said. 'On an estuary where two small rivers join to form a harbour. A little peninsula shelters it from Doubtless Bay and my house is on the peninsula.'

'Set in pohutukawa trees,' she said, her voice dulcet and guileless.

'All the clichés,' he agreed blandly.

'It sounds idyllic. How far from the nearest café?'

The glacial depths of his eyes were lit by a spark of humour. 'Twenty minutes.'

'Too far for me, alas.'

Smiling, she turned with—she hoped—well-hidden relief as Marcus Fielding came up. Marcus was a bit of a pain, but easy to deal with. Kear Lannion's penetrating gaze made her feel as though she had to screen every word, every nuance.

'Janny, darling, how are you?' Marcus kissed her soundly, keeping one arm looped around her shoulders as he held out his other hand to Kear. 'How are you, Kear? Haven't seen you for months. Have you been overseas?'

'I've been busy,' Kear said, shaking the hand he was offered. He smiled, his striking face confident and compelling. 'I see you won the Bremner Prize. Congratulations.'

Marcus grinned like a schoolboy. 'I'd like to say, oh, it was nothing, but as I struggled and bled and anguished for months to get the sculpture ready I don't feel inclined to,' he said. 'At least it gives me a year when I don't have to worry about money.'

They discussed the award for a few minutes longer before Kear was carried off by Sally to meet some newcomer.

Frowning after the tall figure, Marcus said, 'God, if I could get him to buy something of mine I'd be made.'

'I thought he was a farmer.'

'Darling,' Marcus said with affectionate malice, 'of course he is. He's also something of a Renaissance man, is Kear Lannion. Actually, the farm is a thumping great station, but I doubt very much whether it's his sole source of income. I've heard that he owns quite large chunks of various business and enterprises. I know for certain he's a director of several companies. Rumour has it he's got a lot of disposable cash. And he likes to spend some of it on art.'

Jan thought she hid her surprise rather well, but Marcus crowed, 'Ah, you thought he was a philistine, didn't you? Shame on you, darling, all your little prejudices are found out. When he buys, the *cognoscenti* start sniffing around.'

Jan said brightly, 'Well, in that case let's hope he likes your stuff.'

She had allowed herself to fall into a fairly obvious trap. Kear Lannion was not a man you could slot into a comfortable niche and expect to stay there. She wouldn't make that mistake again.

With a swift, sideways look, Marcus purred, 'He has a reputation in other things too.'

Jan stared at him. It was unlike him to be coy; shocking people for the sheer wicked fun of it was more his style.

'Don't we all?' she said neutrally.

'Ladies love him,' Marcus said. 'He likes them too, if they're tall and willowy and beautiful.'

Only four inches shorter than Kear Lannion, not unhandsome, very smartly dressed and with his full mouth set in a modish sneer, he was no match for Kear's effortless male magnetism. And he knew it.

Jan said cheerfully, 'Perhaps you should produce some tall, willowy, beautiful pieces of sculpture for him.'

Laughing, he surprised her by kissing her on the mouth. 'Jan, you're incurably nice. Ah, he's coming back. If I leave you alone, will you sing my praises to him?'

She began to tell him he'd got things wrong, but he grinned and headed off, leaving her caught, as defenceless as a possum on the road at night, in Kear's dispassionate gaze.

'Is he your lover?' Kear asked coolly.

Startled by his unexpected crudeness, she snapped, 'No, he is not.'

Although discretion warned her to be careful, her pulses raced with a keener, more eager beat. Her reaction, half excitement, half antipathy, bewildered her, because she'd never responded to a man like this before. It wasn't as though she had anything to base her dislike on either. Kear was interesting to talk to, with a presence that made him an asset at any social occasion; apparently he was also a worthy member of society and an honest businessman.

She was being absurdly sensitive. Clutching precariously at her temper, she said, 'Now, is there anyone I can introduce you to?'

He didn't even glance around the room. 'I think I know most people,' he said. 'Sally tells me you're an image consultant. What exactly does that mean?'

There was no sign of emotion in his voice, none revealed in the arrogant contours of his face, but she sensed a note of irony that further irritated already raw nerves. 'Basically, I give people confidence,' she said sweetly.

He raised his brows. 'And how do you train for that?'

'I worked in fashion for a while, and then I became intrigued because some people seemed to know instinctively what suited them, whereas others didn't have a clue. I started to read up about it, but there wasn't much to be learnt here, so I had to go to America to find someone who knew what he was doing in the field. When I came back to New Zealand three years ago I decided to set up for myself.'

'You'd be the perfect person,' he said.

It should have been a compliment. However, some primitive sense picked up the meaning of words he wasn't saying, of expressions he controlled, and she said without

knowing why, 'I hear you have an excellent collection
of art.'

He made no modest disclaimer. 'I think so,' he said.
'Marcus was very enthusiastic.'

His mouth curved in a smile that conveyed amusement
without softening its naturally hard line. 'I buy what I
like,' he said. 'He has talent, but he still feels that
emotion and desire are all-important. When he develops
discipline I might buy from him.'

She said firmly, 'I think he has a great future.'

'It will be interesting to see,' he said.

She caught Gerry's eye. Muscles she hadn't known
were tense relaxed as her cousin moved in with her at-
tendant group of dazzled males, saying cheerfully, 'You
look as though you're having a terribly earnest
discussion.'

Jan shook her head. 'Not *earnest*—but definitely
interesting.'

Her cousin beamed up at Kear, who returned her smile
with his overwhelming one.

He was too astute not to know how potent a weapon
that smile was, Jan decided, watching her cousin almost
buckle under its impact. However, Gerry had potent
weapons too. She'd made the phrase 'divinely fair' her
own.

She was tall and willowy as well.

Provoked on some basic level, Jan summoned her best
hostess's smile, made an excuse and left them talking.
Ten minutes later a swift, unnoticed glance revealed that
the men Gerry always collected had drifted off, leaving
Kear Lannion in sole possession.

'You shouldn't let her get away with it,' Great-Aunt
Kit said abruptly. She was Jan's only surviving relative
on her father's side of the family, the sister of her father's
mother. They were seated in armchairs under the pepper
tree, enjoying the warm, rose-scented air.

Jan grinned. 'Gerry's been getting away with it all her life,' she said cheerfully. 'She can't help it. As well as being gorgeous she's nice. Anyway, he's not mine.'

'Time you thought of getting married.'

'I've decided to follow your example,' Jan said, smiling at her aunt, who'd never made any secret of her satisfaction with her single state.

'Well, I've enjoyed my life, I don't deny it, but I think you were made for marriage.'

'I haven't met the right man,' Jan said, stifling a little sigh.

From the edge of the terrace there came a muted peal of laughter from Cynthia. Great-Aunt Kit said, 'There's no such thing. Look at your mother. She adored your father but she couldn't be more happy than she is with Stephen.'

'I wish I'd known my father.'

'Hugo was a charming scamp,' her aunt said acidly. 'He broke his father's heart and then he did the same to your mother's. He might have grown up if he hadn't died on that racetrack, but I doubt it.'

'I remember him—just isolated incidents,' Jan said wistfully. 'And I know my grandfather used to sing nursery rhymes with me. It would have been nice if he'd stayed in New Zealand.'

Her aunt snorted. 'He couldn't bear to see Hugo's eyes in your face. A fine excuse for running away to Australia!'

'I'd like to know more about your side of the family.'

'There wasn't much to know about Hugo beyond the fact that he had more charm than was good for him, and the only family he had was a doting father who couldn't endure his grief. Fergus even blamed your mother for letting Hugo race, when he knew perfectly well it was impossible to stop him from doing whatever he wanted to!'

Jan hadn't known this. She said indignantly, 'What a nerve!'

'He has that, does Fergus Morrison. Ah, well, he adored your father—I suppose it was understandable. He was middle-aged when he married Betsy, and they only ever had Hugo.' Her voice softened as it always did when she mentioned her only sister, who'd died in childbirth.

Oddly enough, it wasn't her father but the restrained figure of her grandfather that Jan had missed the most. She used to wonder why they had both gone, leaving her alone with a mother who had wept for months. Perhaps, she thought now, it had been her memories of the family they'd been that had led her to long so desperately for another. Curiously, she asked, 'Was there no one else? No aunts or uncles or cousins?'

'Not a one. We had no relatives in New Zealand, and I think Fergus had lost touch with his too.'

Carefully avoiding the part of the room where Kear Lannion stood, Jan looked around. 'Family's important,' she said softly.

'You're a nice girl,' her great-aunt said with unexpected force.

Jan kissed her cheek. 'Thank you.'

'You look like Cynthia, but you've got Betsy's eyes. Set on the merest slant, and that bright, intense blue. Now, go on; you don't want to sit here talking to me all night. Here comes Cynthia—you go and enjoy yourself. I want to hear all the gossip, and your mother won't tell me any if you're here.'

Laughing, Jan left them. It was a good party. She looked around in case someone was in trouble, but everyone in the noisy, laughing, chattering crowd appeared to be enjoying themselves without any help from her.

Then Kear Lannion walked down the steps and came across the lawn. She felt her smile tremble, and before it died forced herself to produce another.

'Hello,' she said, wondering if she'd overemphasised her bright tone. 'Can I get you something?'

The thick dark lashes that curled around his pale eyes screened his thoughts too well. She couldn't read him at all, and this made her uneasy because normally she was good at body language.

'You can talk to me,' he said, a hint of irony in his words. 'You've done your duty.'

'What shall we talk about?'

His mouth tightened, then eased into a lazy, almost insolent smile. 'Your innermost secrets,' he said gravely.

Jan's brows shot up. 'Not after such a short acquaintanceship,' she said, just as seriously, wishing that she could hide behind curtains of long hair like some of her young cousins. Smiling, she parried his hard, intent gaze and said, 'Tell me about your farm.'

Yes, that sounded fine—interested but not prying, and social rather than personal. But when she looked up at him, she noticed with a faint quiver in her stomach the speculative gleam in his glance.

'I breed and run beef cattle on Doubtless Bay. Have you ever been up there?'

'It's quite close to Kaitaia, isn't it? I've flown there several times to take seminars and workshops,' she said, trying not to sound indignant. 'And I've sailed around the Bay of Islands.'

His mouth tilted. 'Let me guess. You went on a gin palace and saw all the sights from the deck.'

Ruffled by the amusement in his voice, she bent down to snap off the suede-soft bloom of a gardenia and held it to her nose. Erotic, disturbing, the scent of the flower floated like an offering to unknown gods on the humid air.

She lowered it and said, 'It was definitely a gin palace, but I did go ashore a couple of times.' She didn't care what he thought of her—after all, he was nobody, a mere passer-by in her life.

Kear glanced across to her mother, now walking with Great-Aunt Kit down her favourite border, pointing out flowering treasures. Lights in the garden illuminated them—the tall old woman, the smaller, younger one unobtrusively lending a supporting hand. 'After meeting your mother, I can see where you got your features from. You don't have her eyes, though.'

'Apparently I inherited mine from my father's mother,' she said evenly, thinking it odd for this conversation to turn up twice on the same evening.

'So intense a blue they make me think of the sheen on steel,' he said, and held out his hand for the gardenia.

Startled, she gave it to him and watched as he smelled it, his dark features etched arrogantly against the lights.

The compliment unnerved her totally, melting the bones at the base of her spine. 'Really?' she said in a quiet, startled voice.

'Yes.' His brief smile sent her heart thudding. 'My cousin said that you're Anet Carruthers' sister. I saw her win gold at the Olympics. You're not in the least alike.'

'We're half-sisters. Anet gets her javelin-throwing expertise from my stepfather.' Jan sent a swift, winged smile across to Stephen Carruthers. Obeying a distress signal she hadn't realised she'd sent, he said a few smiling words to the couple he was with and came down to join her.

After that it was easy. Listening to them as they talked, Jan was surprised to find out that Stephen liked Kear; her stepfather was clever and an excellent judge of character, yet he responded to the other man's magnetism without any sign of resistance. But what set her stupid heart galloping in an uneven rhythm was the sight of that gardenia tucked negligently into Kear's buttonhole.

'Interesting chap, Lannion—I've always liked him,' Stephen said hours later, when all the guests had gone.

'I didn't realise you knew him,' Jan murmured.

'He's on a couple of boards with me. Not an easy chap to know, and no one pushes him around, but he's a good man to have beside you in a fight.'

Cynthia nodded. 'As well as being a very desirable piece of real estate.'

'Mother!' Jan pretended to be shocked.

Laughing, her mother defended her choice of words. 'That's what Gerry called him. I think she might be smitten.'

Jan subdued something that came ominously close to being jealousy, and kissed her parents. 'Well, I'm heading off. Goodnight, and thank you. I had a lovely party.'

'You're sure you don't want to stay the night?' her mother asked automatically.

'No, I'll go home, thanks.' Jan hid a yawn. 'I'll see you tomorrow morning, though. And don't have the place cleaned up by the time I get here like you did last year!'

'There's not a lot to do, darling. The caterers have already tidied up, so all that's necessary is a bit of vacuuming.'

'Don't do it.' Jan looked at her stepfather. 'Dad, keep her in bed.'

His answering grin was transformed into laughter as Cynthia blushed and bridled and shook her finger at him.

She was very lucky, Jan thought as she drove through Auckland's darkened streets. She had a super family.

Back at home, she took off her make-up before sitting on the side of the bed with Anet's present in her lap. She had been astounded when she'd opened it, because the tiny painting on ivory had been given to Anet by mutual friends barely a year before.

Even the note hadn't allayed her surprise. Anet had written:

Dearest Jan

I hope you have a wonderful birthday. I'm sorry we won't be there—I always hate missing your party, the best of the year! This is our present. Yes, I know Olivia and Drake gave the portrait to me, but it was always with the proviso that I had to hand her on sooner or later. She's ready to leave now, and I want you to have her. Don't worry about her; she has the ability to keep herself out of trouble. Jan, be happy.

Jan tilted the severe wooden frame so that the light illuminated the pretty face. It was exquisite work, done by a master. Fresh as though she were not at least two hundred years old, the woman gazed serenely out at the world, her delicately fine features set in an expression of confident assurance.

'I wonder just what she means when she says you're ready to leave now,' Jan murmured. 'I wish you could tell me. I'll look after you carefully, and when Anet comes back I'll ask her why she was so cryptic.' Carefully, she steadied the wooden frame and put it on her dressing table.

Two weeks later Jan was ushered into a solicitor's office in the city. Holding out her hand, she said, 'Mr Gates? I'm Jan Carruthers.'

He was a well-tailored, middle-aged man, with shrewd dark eyes and a mouth clamped shut on secrets. 'How do you do, Ms Carruthers,' he said neutrally. 'Actually, I think that legally your surname is Morrison, is it not?'

'No,' she said a little stiffly. 'My stepfather adopted me.'

'I see.'

'But my birth father was Hugo Morrison.'

He nodded. 'Do sit down, Ms Carruthers,' he said, and gestured to a chair. He waited until she was seated before saying smoothly, 'Thank you for responding so promptly to my letter. You have your birth certificate?'

'I have my shortened adoption one,' she said, handing it over. 'I can write away and get a copy of the one with my father's name on it if you want it.'

'It might be a good idea, but this will do for the moment.' He looked at the document, then passed it back to her, saying, 'Ms Carruthers, are you aware that you had a paternal grandfather—your birth father's father?'

'Yes,' she said, feeling something chilly take up residence in the pit of her stomach. 'Fergus Morrison. He went to Australia after my father's death.'

'He returned to New Zealand about fifteen years ago,' he said.

Astonishment raised her voice. 'Did he?'

'Yes.' He shuffled the papers on his desk a moment before saying, 'He saw you at some function a few years ago.'

She felt the colour leach from her face. 'Why didn't he speak to me?' she asked numbly.

'I gather he thought he might not be welcome,' he said, watching her with keen interest.

'He might have tried to find out.'

'I'm afraid I don't know what his reasons were for keeping his distance. However, he made this will after he'd seen you.'

He paused, but she'd already guessed what he was going to say. She'd never have thought that it could hurt so much.

'Ms Carruthers, your grandfather died a year ago. He wanted his estate wound up before you were contacted. That has now been done, leaving money and a hundred acres of land some hundred or so miles north of Whangarei, in Northland. As you are your grandfather's sole beneficiary, it is yours.'

She shook her head. 'I don't want it,' she said. Her voice sounded odd, as though she had a severe cold.

'There is no one else.' He was firm. 'If you don't accept it, it will be sold and everything will go into the Consolidated Fund. There is, however, a condition.'

'What?' she asked warily.

He picked out a piece of paper. 'There is a house on the property. He wanted you to stay there for a month before you decide what to do.'

'That's impossible. I have a business to run.'

'You have a year's grace. After you've fulfilled his wish you can do what you like with the property.' He looked at her with something like compassion in those cautious eyes. 'There is quite a lot of money involved, Ms Carruthers,' he said.

'Exactly how much?'

'Well, the place itself is on the coast. I believe there are several beaches. People are prepared to pay a considerable amount of money for coastal property nowadays,' he said calmly.

Slowly she asked, 'And if I don't stay there everything goes to the government?'

'I'm afraid so.'

Jan thought of the centre. She could sell this unexpected inheritance and use the money to buy land closer to Auckland for a camp. Or perhaps, she thought, excitement quickening inside her, it would be suitable in itself for such an enterprise. At the very least, its sale would give the centre money to buy a van and add to the trust fund.

Compared to that, a month out of her life wasn't much sacrifice. She'd allowed herself a fortnight's holiday in May, and with a little shuffling she could probably take a whole month.

Instantly making up her mind, she said, 'All right. If I decide I want this land, do I have to stay there the whole time? I mean, can I make dashes to Auckland overnight?'

'Certainly,' he said gravely.

She nodded. 'And exactly where is this place?'

'Reasonably close to Mangonui,' he said. 'It's a very scenic area. The property has frontage on Doubtless Bay.'

'Good heavens,' she said blankly.

'Does that make a difference?'

'No. No—no difference at all. You don't happen to know who the neighbours are, do you?'

He shuffled more papers. 'There's only one—a Mr Kear Lannion. Well-known in the north—an excellent farmer—and, I understand, prominent in business circles both here and in Australia.'

As she went away Jan thought it was very strange that she should meet a man one week and within the next fortnight find herself committed to a month's stay next door to him.

And she would not, she told herself, firmly squelching something that could have been an eager, forbidden anticipation, consider that it might be some sort of omen— that it might be *meant*.

Six weeks later she drove the MG carefully down a narrow road beside a harbour formed by the estuaries of two small rivers. Black tarmac wound ahead of her. Across an expanse of glinting water the main north road bypassed the little village of Mangonui to head for Kaitaia. She could see what was probably the peninsula where Kear lived, a hilly appendage separating the harbour from the huge, open Doubtless Bay beyond. Within the protective embrace of pohutukawa trees were tantalising glimpses of a double-storeyed house.

On the neck of the peninsula the land crouched to reveal a glimpse of kingfisher-blue sea. Somewhere on a beach below that dip stood her grandfather's house. Inland, a vast area of hilly green farmland crumpled eventually into the foothills of a high bush-covered peak.

By some quirk of settlement the only access to her grandfather's land was across Kear Lannion's property.

'That's odd, surely?' she'd said to her stepfather, before he and Cynthia had left for a holiday in Fiji.

'Very,' he'd answered drily. 'I imagine there's some form of easement across Lannion's land.'

The road finished at what was obviously the entrance to Kear's farm. A notice proclaimed that it was called Papanui, and five letter-boxes indicated a surprisingly large workforce. Jan stopped and examined them in case one had her grandfather's name on it. None did.

She stood looking around, breathing in the sharp, sea-scented air, smiling a little as she recalled the swift glint in Kear's eyes when she'd teased him about the quality of rural air. A cattlestop kept animals within while allowing vehicles through without the bother of opening and closing a gate. On the edge of the road an old rosebush scrambled in an untidy heap over a bank that revealed the shells of cockles, washed bone-white by rain and sun. An ancient Maori midden, probably.

Jan drew an unsteady breath and got back into the car. After some careful driving through what even to her city eyes were obviously fertile paddocks, she came to a place where the road divided; obeying her instructions, she took the right-hand fork. Immediately the surface of the road deteriorated into a series of ruts as it plunged down through a thick forest of feathery kanuka trees.

'It's all right,' she comforted the MG. 'Not much longer now.'

But it seemed to go on for ever, gouged into deeper and deeper furrows by the same rains that had produced the lush green grass on Kear Lannion's station. Jan changed gear so cautiously that she felt she was on tiptoe, and finally, after creeping down a last steep grade, emerged onto a swathe of what had once been grass but was now reverting rapidly to coastal teatree scrub.

'Oh, my God,' she said as she saw the house.

She stopped on a final flourish of white road metal and, half-horrified, half-delighted, got out of the car.

The flat area, about three acres of it, was cradled by hills and bordered by a beach of white sand. To one side of the bay a little stream debouched into the sea. So far, so good. However, on the other side of the stream mangroves crouched, olive-green and sinister, their gnarled roots anchoring them into mud that seemed to have a life of its own, if the furtive movements she could see from the corners of her eyes were any indication.

'Oh, hell,' she said aloud, repressing a shiver. It looked the sort of place that should have crocodiles lying in wait.

Worse even than that was the house, an old weatherboard bach left over from the days when families used to camp out all summer in such affairs, with a large brick chimney supporting the end wall. Further back from the beach, and on higher ground, stood a floorless, three-sided shed clad in sheets of rusting corrugated iron. The two buildings looked forlorn and dingy and lonely, a jarring note in the serenity of sea and sky.

'Why,' Jan asked herself aloud, 'don't you listen when people tell you you're too impetuous for your own good? And why on earth did he want me to spend a whole month here?'

Tears sprang to her eyes. No man should have to live in conditions like this when he was old and death not far away. The fact that her grandfather had chosen it didn't help.

She fished out a handkerchief and wiped her eyes before heading determinedly across the coarse, springy grass towards the bach, the key to the door in her hand.

'It's highly unlikely,' the solicitor had told her as he'd handed it over, 'that it needs locking. However, your grandfather was a careful man.'

Careful? Jan nearly laughed. Anyone who lived in this shack had to be positively reckless! It looked ready to collapse at any minute.

It should have been impossible, but the inside was even worse than the exterior. Dust lay squalidly on the few items of old furniture and coated every other surface. Mixed with salt and rain-stains on the windows, it was so thick that she could only just see through the panes.

Jan was standing in the middle of the main room, looking helplessly around, when she heard the sound of an engine. It startled her so much that she scanned the room desperately, searching for a place to hide.

'Don't be an idiot!' she commanded stoutly. But she stood out of sight as a Land Rover came down the hill, considerably faster than she had, and pulled to a stop beside her car, so incongruously sporty and chic.

Jan's heart thumped erratically in her chest. She'd recognise that lithe form anywhere.

At Kear Lannion's curt command the black and white dog on the back of his vehicle stopped its eager suggestions that it get down and explore and settled back quietly, its eyes fixed on him as he came towards the house.

He could be an axe murderer, but at that moment he represented safety. The oppressive weight of her grandfather's fate lifted slightly as Jan walked across the cracked linoleum floor-covering to stand in the doorway.

'Hello,' he said, looking, she saw with a spurt of anger, unsurprised, although the narrowed grey eyes were enigmatic. 'This is a long way from Auckland.'

'Isn't it just? Another universe.' The flippancy of her reply sounded crudely out of place, but it was all she could manage.

He smiled, not very nicely. That comprehensive survey had taken in her narrow linen trousers and elegant boots, the fine weave of her cotton shirt and the thin gold chain around her neck.

'This is private property,' he said.

Jan discovered that she disliked him in equal measure to her unbidden, reluctant attraction to him. '*My* private property,' she told him, not without relish.

He didn't move but she detected a waiting kind of stillness in him, an unexpressed astonishment. Aha, she thought maliciously, you didn't know that.

Not even trying to hide the dismissive note in his words, he said, 'How did this happen?'

'Fergus Morrison was my grandfather.'

His brows came together. For a moment she sensed a cold, deliberate patience that sent an icy chill down her back.

Then he said, 'I see. I assume you plan to sell it.'

Later, she would understand that that was when she'd made up her mind to keep the place, but at the time she was too busy trying to ignore his effect on her to realise anything. 'Possibly,' she said.

It was just his size; short, thin people tended to be a bit wary of big people, especially when those big people walked with head erect and a rangy, almost arrogant self-assurance that sent out all sorts of messages—most of them tinged with intimidating overtones.

Kear went on conversationally, 'If you do, I'd like first refusal.'

It didn't seem too much to give him, but something held her back. She said, 'I'll have to talk to my solicitor about that.'

'Of course,' he said laconically. Nothing altered in his expression, no emotion darkened the pale gaze, but every nerve in her body suddenly screamed a warning.

He said, 'Where do you plan to stay the night?'

As wary as a deer in tiger-haunted jungle, she swallowed. 'Here.'

There was an alarming silence. Or perhaps it was stunned. No, a swift upward glance revealed that the first word had been the right one. Kear Lannion kept tight rein on his emotions, but his mouth had compressed and there was a glint of irritation in the frigid depths of his eyes.

'Do you know how to work the range? The water?'

'No,' she said.

With brusque impatience he demanded, 'Don't you think it would have been a good idea to find out what the conditions were before you came up to gloat over your inheritance?'

Jan raised her brows, delicately questioning his right to make such comments. 'I'll manage.'

His icy gaze slid across her face, cold enough to burn the ivory skin. She thought she actually felt the welts as he said, 'So, even though you never came near Fergus Morrison, he left what he had to you when he died?'

'He did.' It angered her that this man somehow managed to strip off the comfortingly opaque social mask she took for granted. She never lost her temper—*never*—and yet she wanted to stamp her feet and scream with childish, uncontrolled rage. In a voice that could have congealed lava she told him, 'I'm his only descendant, apparently. I thought he was dead—we all did. He left for Australia after my father died, and didn't contact us when he came back.'

'I wonder why?'

'My mother told me he adored my father and went a little mad when he was killed.'

'He certainly turned into a hermit,' he said. 'Jan, you can't stay here. You'd better come back and spend the night at my place.'

CHAPTER THREE

'THAT'S very kind of you,' Jan said formally, 'but I'll be perfectly all right.'

Sleeping with rats—and oh, how she prayed there weren't any around!—would be less stressful than accepting his hospitality.

His dark brows drew together above hard eyes. 'I've seen you in your native habitat,' he said, 'and you are not going to like it here, believe me.'

She didn't have to prove herself—she wasn't in the least worried about what he thought of her—and she wasn't going to cave in like a wimp under the relentless assault of his masculine dominance.

Tilting her chin, she said, 'I'll be perfectly all right.' Wickedly, she added, 'I have been camping several times.'

And she enjoyed a fierce satisfaction when his mouth curved into a slow smile that was both sinister and sexy as hell.

'Don't play games with me,' he said softly. 'There's a difference between camping with the latest equipment and this. You'll find the homestead much more comfortable.'

It would be perilously easy to give in to that deep, assured voice, to his smooth assumption of mastery—especially as that smile sent a hot pulse of sensation washing through her. Ignoring the quick, uneven flurry of her heartbeats, Jan said crisply, 'I'm sure I would, but I'm quite capable of looking after myself.'

He gave her another intent, measuring glance, then said, 'If you're determined to stay here I'll leave you my mobile phone.'

Lightly, wishing he'd go, Jan told him, 'I have one in the car. Look, if it worries you, give me your number and I'll call each night to let you know I'm all right.'

He didn't like being crossed. Not that he showed it—she was beginning to think that his control over his expression was almost unnatural—but she could feel the irritation coming off him in waves. His disapproval stiffened her backbone—not ousting the intense awareness that played havoc with her heartbeat, but making it easier to ignore.

He seemed to realise that she meant it, because he said indifferently, 'Very well, if that's what you want.' And he gave her his number, waiting while she wrote it down in her Filofax.

'Ring tonight at seven,' he said. 'Have you got food?'

'Yes, plenty, thanks.'

'I'll see you around.' And he turned and went back to the Land Rover, the warm autumn sun striking fire from his head.

She watched him turn the vehicle with an economy of movement she envied; a hand waved, the dog braced itself and the Land Rover took the rutted track easily and without fuss to disappear beneath the kanuka trees.

Perhaps she should have asked him how to get the range going. Ah, well, it was too late now, and she was intelligent enough to work it out on her own. Waiting until the sound of the engine had died away, she drove the scarlet MG into the shed, where it would be sheltered from any rain. Looking around at the logs neatly stacked against the walls, she decided that the range had to be fuelled by wood.

Somehow, from there the bach looked even more suspicious and surly. 'It's only because you could have gone to stay with the local laird,' she said out loud, forcing herself to walk back across the coarse grass.

Once inside she explored properly. There was no kitchen, just a rickety set of cupboards—empty, she was thankful to discover. An old enamel bowl, probably used for washing-up as there was no sink, rested upside down on a bench, hiding three dead spiders and the faded pattern of a vinyl covering. A small window revealed a galvanised tank on a dilapidated wooden stand just a few feet away; from it one pipe led to a tap, another to the lean-to bathroom at the back of the bach.

In which, she was grateful to see, there was a proper toilet. No chilly morning trips to an outdoor privy.

First things first. She tried the tap over the bath and only realised how tense she'd been when water spurted into the bottom and she felt overwhelming relief. Even then, she didn't draw a breath until the year's accumulation of debris in the pipe drained away and the water ran clear. Although it looked as though the only method of heating it was the range, at least she wasn't going to have to carry water to the bach in buckets.

She turned the tap off and went to check out the bedroom.

It was lined with matchboarding, and an old double bed with wirewove and kapok mattress that smelt sourly of dampness took up most of the room. Gingerly, Jan opened the door of a kauri wardrobe to find that someone had cleared everything away there too.

Wondering just what Fergus Morrison had hoped to achieve with the conditional clause in his will, she went back to the main room. A rocking chair in front of the range and an unpainted wooden table and chair pushed against the wall beneath the window were its sole items of furniture.

But the view from the window stopped the breath in her throat. Long, mellow rays from the afternoon sun illuminated the panorama with an artist's skilful hand, glinted across the beach, turned the still waters to a sheet of softly glowing pearl-blue. In the light's fugitive glamour even the mangroves looked a little less sinister.

'Yes,' she said aloud, imagining buildings on the flat land and the voices of children and adolescents—young lives given hope and confidence, 'it could be *perfect*.'

She'd brought detergents and rags, and after changing into jeans and T-shirt she wasted a good half-hour fiddling around with kindling and paper in the firebox of the range, juggling levers and knobs only to have each promising fire die down into raw-smelling ashes. Eventually she gave up in disgust, and, thanking the twentieth century for detergents, scrubbed the porcelain bath with cold water before tackling the other fittings. They were not as old as the bath or the building, so presumably her grandfather had had them installed fifteen years ago, when he'd come to live here.

She wasn't going to be able to clean everything before it got dark, so she left the walls and merely swept the floors. They'd be easier to clean when she'd worked out how to get hot water. She dragged both chairs and the table into the sunlight, scrubbing them and leaving them to dry while she ventured back into the bedroom.

Wrinkling her nose, she discarded the kapok mattress, dumping it where a circle of dark ashes beneath long, thrusting tendrils of some strongly growing grass revealed a bonfire site.

Fortunately she'd borrowed a double inflatable mattress from a friend. It wouldn't be particularly comfortable, but it smelt better and would be much more conducive to a good night's sleep than the horror she'd found on the bed.

So Kear Lannion wanted first refusal on the land, did he? Smiling limpidly, Jan imagined his face when she told him she wasn't selling. And how would he respond when she told him she planned to turn it into a camp for at-risk girls? She wondered whether he'd take his defeat graciously. Men accustomed to getting their own way usually didn't, but Kear was different; his armour of self-control had no visible weaknesses.

He would, she decided with an inner spark of excitement, fight fair, but he'd fight.

It was almost dusk when at last she brought the furniture back inside and unpacked the car. For some reason she'd brought the little portrait Anet and Lucas had given her, but one look at the smiling, perfect countenance of the unknown woman made her laugh.

'You look utterly, completely, totally out of place,' she said, returning her to the suede bag that protected her and putting her back in her case. Like Jan's clothes, she could stay there until she'd cleaned the wardrobe and its drawers.

While she pumped up the mattress dusk came galloping silently in—a moment's hesitation between the warm light of day and the pellucid darkness of night. Apprehensively Jan peered at the lamp. She hadn't lied to Kear; years ago she'd gone camping with friends who had used a hurricane lamp for light. Unfortunately, beyond recalling that it had been tricky to deal with, she couldn't remember what you did with it.

'Hope for a full moon,' she told herself.

But in case there wasn't one she washed all over in cold water, rubbed away the shivers with her towel and donned a clean T-shirt and trousers before constructing a sandwich and eating it at the table.

Through the open windows she watched the light die out of the sky and the swift arrival of night, made fragrant by the tang of salt and the balsam of the kanuka trees, and another, more exotic perfume, almost tropical in its exuberance. Tomorrow, she promised herself, she'd find the flower that scented the air so deliciously.

Apart from the faint crowns of stars no light brightened the sky, not even the tiny promise of a new moon. Fortunately Jan never travelled without a torch. However, its light seemed meagre and easily used up, so she flicked it off and sat down in the humid darkness, looking out over the unseen bay.

Although the hard work of cleaning the bach out had tired her, she basked in a glow of satisfaction. For a moment she thought she could see why her grandfather had decided to live there.

Until, as if answering some subliminal cue, mosquitoes poured inside in battalions, whining hatefully around her head and shoulders, settling with blood-sucking eagerness on her exposed skin. Muttering curses, Jan leapt to her feet and wrenched the windows closed. One thing she hadn't thought to bring was fly spray. With another string of unladylike oaths she dived for the sponge-bag where she kept insect repellent.

By then it was too dark to see the wretched things. Only their ominous, maddening noise revealed their presence—that and the thousands of bites she imagined she could feel. Smothering her skin with the liquid, she resigned herself to the inevitable and climbed into the embrace of her sleeping bag.

Grimly, she tried to relax.

It proved difficult, because as well as suffering heat and mosquitoes she kept going over her meeting with Kear Lannion, thinking of the things she could have said to him—witty, intelligent remarks that would have made him realise that she wasn't a silly twit with no more sense than to overdress at the polo and cause a nasty incident that could have killed her and the horse, not to mention the horse's rider. It wasn't like her to be almost tongue-tied; she'd always been rather proud of her fund of conversation.

Oh, well, pride goes before a fall, she told herself. It's good for your soul.

Her mind summoned a vivid recollection of the exciting way Kear's mouth curled when he smiled. No, that was dangerous. Much better to remember the latent darkness of antagonism that had sparked his attitude. He didn't like her. Well, she didn't like him either, so there was no reason to feel hurt.

He had an unsettling effect on her. Whatever she felt, it was more than the casual appreciation of a woman for an intensely masculine man, and nothing could be allowed to come of it.

Scratching every so often, she slipped into sleep.

And woke from deep unconsciousness into terror, lying rigid, with her brain struggling to discern what exactly had woken her.

A noise, she thought with drugged lethargy.

A noise she had never heard before.

She held her breath, listening. All she could hear were several mosquitoes preparing to divebomb her, until after nerve-shattering minutes a menacing, inhuman chattering erupted just outside the bedroom window. Jan's breath blocked her throat; fear, primeval and unharnessed, kicked her in the stomach.

Forcefully subduing the incipient panic, she tried to think logically. It couldn't be an animal—no animal in New Zealand had a cry like that. A bird? Surely that noise hadn't come from a bird's throat! The radio station she listened to each morning played birdcalls before the news. Locked in stasis on the bed, she tried to remember if she'd ever heard anything like that.

No, it wasn't a sound you'd forget.

Forcing herself to breathe, to whip her sluggish mind into action, she went through the possibilities. Rats, perhaps. But rats squeaked. Hedgehogs—she'd heard them snuffle, but this was no snuffle.

It couldn't be a human. Repressing stupid fears culled from a variety of horror movies and novels, Jan slid down the zip of her sleeping bag. Only marginally cooler than she was, sticky, heavy air pressed onto her goosebumps. She wished she slept in pyjamas—even a nightgown would have been some sort of protection from whatever lay in wait outside. Thank God she'd shut the windows against the mosquitoes, so whatever it was couldn't get inside.

Fortunately she'd dropped her dressing gown on the end of the bed. Moving with painful hesitance, and as silently as she could with limbs weighted by terror, she huddled it around her and tiptoed across to the pale rectangle of the window, keeping well to one side. Her heart thumped loudly in her chest, blocking out any other noise.

It wasn't pitch-dark; arrayed in their impersonal stations, the constellations glittered coldly down. In their light she could make out the beach, the dense line of the mangroves, the star-shimmer across the harbour but nothing else, no movement, no darker shape in the grass.

Gradually her breathing steadied, her heart slowed to its normal pace. She turned away from the window.

And at that moment the noise came again.

Panic spun up her spine, liquidised her brain. She found herself pushing the back of her hand against her mouth to keep back a scream, felt the strain of her dilating eyes as she searched the long grass for whatever thing was making that noise. Horrified, she realised she was trembling.

Calm down this minute, she commanded herself. For heaven's sake, woman, it has to be some form of night-life, and therefore perfectly safe. There's nothing but man to be afraid of in the New Zealand countryside, and no human makes that sound.

Get the torch.

And then another noise broke the heavy silence, the faint thrum of an engine. At first she thought it was a boat, but a sudden brilliant cone of light on the wall whipped her head around. Somebody was coming down the hill, and it could only be one person.

By the time Kear had got out of the Land Rover and was at the door she had unlocked it. She didn't dare speak—if she opened her mouth she'd babble hysterically she thought—but she had never been so glad to see anyone in her life.

The moment the light from his torch fastened onto her face he demanded, 'What the hell's going on?'

Eyes held shut, Jan shook her head.

'You're as white as a sheet. Did I frighten you? Jan, tell me!'

'A noise,' she muttered, clamping down on her fear and her relief.

'Where?'

'Outside.' She jerked her head. 'On the beach, I think.'

She fell back before him as he came in with silent, terrifying speed. Soundlessly he closed the door behind him and stood listening. The faint click as he switched off the torch echoed in her ears. With night-attuned eyes, Jan looked up at the arrogant angles of his face, the wide shoulders and muscled forearms, the big body held motionless with the coiled patience of disciplined strength.

Jan had always been independent, had never needed anyone to look after her, nor wanted to be cared for and cosseted. She'd been the one who'd looked after others. Yet for a second she appreciated the seductive pleasure of being dependent. Now that he was here she was no longer afraid.

He said so quietly that she had to strain to hear, 'Get over by the wall. I want to look out of the window.'

When she didn't immediately move he put his hands on her shoulders and set her out of his way, saying in that same almost noiseless, unhurried voice, 'It's all right, I won't let anything hurt you.'

It took Jan a moment or two to realise what he'd said. Well, what had she expected? Behave like a wimp and that's what you get taken for.

He was a dark shadow against the wall, filling her sight, filling her mind, waiting with a predator's inexorable singleness of purpose. Jan's hand clenched between her breasts, her embarrassment giving way to an emotion she didn't recognise.

After a tense silence he said, 'I can't see anything. Anyway, almost certainly the Land Rover will have frightened it away. Tell me what this noise sounded like.'

As best she could, she imitated it.

'Ah,' he said gravely, 'that was a possum.'

'A possum?' Furious with herself, furious with him for so carefully not laughing, she said, 'I didn't know they made a noise.'

'A variety of them, actually. Just wait until they get on the roof. They sound like bears.'

Sick with humiliation, she rallied the rags of her dignity around her. 'Ah, well, I'll know next time. Tell me, what are you doing here at this time of night?'

'It's only nine o'clock,' he said, as though his mind was on something else. 'I came because you said you'd ring and you didn't.'

'Oh.' She felt inexpressibly stupid. 'I forgot,' she said lamely. 'I'm sorry.'

'Don't worry. Why are we standing here in the dark?'

'I don't know how to use the lamp,' she told him with stiff reluctance.

A taut silence stretched between them. He said harshly, 'Or the range, I suppose?'

Her silence was answer enough. 'Get dressed,' he commanded, 'and I'll take you home with me.'

Temptation gave her words bite. 'That's very kind of you, but now that I know what the noises were I'll be perfectly all right.'

'There are other noises,' he said, revealing a casual cruelty that startled her.

'I'm not normally easily frightened,' she retorted, her adrenalin levels rising again, to banish the slow weariness that ached through her. 'I'll be all right. Thank you,' she added with belated good manners.

His laugh was a hard sound, without humour. 'I admire you for trying to stick it out—'

'I'm not *trying*,' she snapped, then sucked in her breath and began again, using her most reasonable tone. 'Look, I know my size tends to make people think I'm not capable of looking after myself, but I've been doing it quite successfully for some years now. I folded tonight, but it won't happen again.'

'How do I know that?' he asked, not attempting to moderate his curtness.

When she gave him no answer he went on remorselessly, 'Have you got a torch?'

She nodded. Clearly he was able to see in the dark, because he asked, 'Why didn't you use it?'

'I—was just getting it when you came down the hill,' she said, not willing to admit that for a few sickening seconds she had succumbed to a hunted creature's instinct to keep still and cower away. Before he had a chance to answer she hurried on, 'Kear, I'm grateful for your help, and yes I was frightened, but I won't be from now on, I assure you.'

It was the truth. She thought with shame of the fancy that had slipped into her brain, that somehow the noise was connected to her grandfather.

'He died in hospital,' Kear said, uncannily reading her mind. 'Not here.'

She said thinly, 'It doesn't matter.'

'Are you usually so bloody obstinate?'

She shrugged. The speculation in his words was underlined by an oblique amusement that made her distinctly uneasy. 'My mother tells me I've been like that from birth,' she said.

'Definitely your grandfather's heir,' he said caustically. 'He was a stubborn, stiff-necked old man, and rather proud of it. Ah, well, if you won't come with me I'll stay here.'

Jan felt her jaw drop. Dry-mouthed, she said, 'There's no place for you to sleep.'

'I know there's a double bed in the other room. And you won't take up much space.'

Did he think that if he threatened her with that she'd give in and go meekly with him? Jan said angrily, 'This is ridiculous! For heaven's sake, Kear, you've done your knight-errant thing, and very grateful I am for it, but I'm perfectly all right now.'

'The choice is yours,' he said, an undertone of steel in the words telling her that he meant it. 'Either you come home with me or I stay here.'

She measured him with angry eyes. By now thoroughly accustomed to the dark, she could see the cool determination in his features, the high-handed, inflexible toughness that warned her she was fighting a losing battle. Both choices of action were equally unpalatable, but there was no way she could get rid of him.

So she called his bluff. 'Then stay here and see if I care,' she snapped, turning around.

Even then she didn't really think he'd do it. But he switched on the torch and, not directing the light at her, followed her into the small bedroom, waiting until she'd zipped herself defiantly into her sleeping bag. Then he sat down on the bed, took off his shoes, and lifted long legs onto the bed beside her.

The air mattress gave beneath his weight. Jan froze. Between her teeth, she stated, 'I do not want you here.'

'Then we go to the homestead,' he said mercilessly.

Beyond thought, she slid from the bed and, clutching her sleeping bag around her, shuffled towards the door.

An imperious hand on her shoulder stopped her. He made no noise when he moved, but he was fast. 'Where are you going?' he asked, his voice cool and quiet and silky.

'I'll sleep in the chair.'

With effortless, infuriating strength he picked her up and dumped her back onto the bed. 'Don't be an idiot,' he said. 'And just in case you feel like wandering around in the night, I sleep very lightly.'

Huddling into the hot folds of her sleeping bag, Jan longed passionately to be twice her size and built like a wrestler, or an adept at some esoteric oriental martial art that would enable her to toss him over her shoulder and see him out of the door. Sheer, frustrated rage smouldered behind her eyelids, burned through her brain and sent a charge of sheer antagonism through her body.

The only thing that stopped her from trying out the defensive tricks she'd learned was her suspicion that he'd be expecting them and more than able to counter them.

Besides, she had to admit that he was keeping well onto his side of the bed. They weren't touching at all, which made her feeling of being confined by him all the more surprising. Mutinously she turned towards the wall and closed her eyes.

Oddly enough, she wasn't afraid. Excited, yes, and racked by an uneasy anticipation which warned her of her vulnerability, but she had no fear that Kear would take advantage of her.

Yet this whole situation was deadly dangerous. She could hear him breathing, smell the faint, musky male scent which set off a mixture of alarm bells and pleasure in her.

'All you have to do,' he said mildly, 'is come home with me. You'll have your own bed—your own room. And I'll bring you back in the morning.'

Oh, it was tempting.

She had almost decided to give in when she thought that if she did, he might expect her to stay at his place from then on. No, if he spent an uncomfortable night here and she stayed determined he'd have to give in. Besides, it was now a matter of pride.

The infuriating buzz of a mosquito whined past her ear. Tranquilly she said, 'Sorry about the wildlife.'

'Mosquitoes don't bother me.'

Of course they wouldn't. His blood probably poisoned them. No doubt he could deal with any wildlife that came his way—wrestle crocodiles with his bare hands if he felt like it. Wishing vengefully that there *were* crocodiles out there in the mangroves, she simmered with thwarted fury as the sleeping bag settled stickily around her.

'Did you know,' he enquired conversationally, 'that New Zealand is the only place in the world that has mangrove swamps without crocodiles?'

She couldn't stop a twitch of astonishment. Could he read her mind? Aloud she snapped, 'I hate men who talk in bed.'

His laughter was soft. 'Poor Jan. Why don't you do the sensible thing?'

'Won't someone be missing you?'

'My housekeeper might tomorrow morning, if she's up before I get home or before I ring to let her know where I am.'

Gritting her teeth, she said, 'I do not respond well to threats.'

'I wasn't threatening you.'

'Oh, yes, you were,' she stated. 'I don't give a damn who you tell that you spent the night here. I don't know anybody here and I don't care. And I despise men who kiss and—' She broke off, feeling unutterably stupid.

Silence hung, throbbing with unspoken words between them.

Kear broke it. 'So do I,' he said calmly. 'And you were right, it was a threat. I'll have to ring my housekeeper reasonably early in the morning so she won't worry, but I won't tell her where I spent the night.'

It wasn't an apology, so she decided to ignore it. 'Don't tell me,' she said acridly, filled with an enormous sense of ill-usage. 'You wake up at six every morning.'

'Around then.'

She said, 'Wake me before seven and I'll have your guts for garters.'

'I'll try not to,' he said. He didn't even try to hide the amusement in his voice, damn him.

Jan huddled deep into her sleeping bag. Her guilt at leaving him out in the cold without a pillow rapidly dissipated as the interior of the sleeping bag heated up. Still clad in her dressing gown, she soon began to sweat.

Her last sensible thought was a prolonged and elaborate curse on the man who lay peacefully beside her. But she dreamed—of drowning in warm milk—until the clammy, unbearable heat was replaced by the warmth of a man's body and the strength of a man's arms about her. After that her dreams were different.

She woke to the delectable scents of bacon and coffee, to sunlight flooding across the room in a sweep of gold and the lazy cry of a seagull as it swung above the bay.

Lying lax and supine against the pillow, filled with an enormous sense of well-being, Jan wondered where she was.

Until memory roared back with all the energy of an express train, and she jerked over onto her back. Through the open bedroom door she could see Kear Lannion's tall figure at the range. Grimacing, she hoped he wouldn't hold a grudge for what she hoped fervently had been a miserable night.

In pleasing contrast to the sticky atmosphere of the previous evening, the air that surged in through the open window was fresh and almost chilly, and blessedly free of insects. Snatches of dreams fluttered through her mind, evanescent as soap bubbles, evaporating even as she tried to grab them. Sitting up, she pushed the sleeping bag back and climbed out.

'Good morning,' Kear said from the doorway.

Absurdly conscious that her dressing gown was old and thin, and that she was sweaty enough to make it too revealing, she froze. However, his eyes stayed fixed to her face.

He might be a pig-headed autocrat, but someone had taught him manners.

'Good morning,' she said shortly, realising just how complete her disadvantage was.

Because he looked magnificent, far better than a man who had spent the night in his clothes should look. Unshaven, his beard dark against the tanned skin of his face, he reminded her of a very healthy pirate. His eyes were clear, the irises an antique, opaque silver, and he looked as though he'd been up for hours and had enjoyed every one of them.

Jan, whose sleep-drugged brain needed caffeine to jog it into action, couldn't stop staring at him. He always looked good, she thought faintly. How did he manage that? Each time she'd seen him he'd outshone every other man; the jodhpurs and shirt at the polo ground had given him a reckless, compelling attraction that the conservatively cut suit he'd worn to her party had only intensified. And this morning the cotton shirt with its sleeves rolled up and the casual trousers proved perfect wear for waking up beside a strange woman.

They weren't even crumpled!

But his clothes didn't give him that overwhelming male magnetism; that came from inside—a combination of forcefulness, intelligence and disciplined self-reliance.

'Go away,' she croaked, shutting her eyes. 'I can't bear people who smile before ten.'

'Wash your face and you'll feel better,' he said heartlessly. 'I used the towel you put out, so you'll need another. Breakfast's in five minutes.'

By some miracle he'd coaxed warm water into the pipes. As she gave herself a quick all-over splash then cleaned her teeth Jan thought gloomily that life simply wasn't fair. She had right on her side and she felt like something a seagull had refused, while he positively reeked of rude good health.

Grumpily, she pulled on a T-shirt and jeans and hung her dressing gown on the old hook behind the door. Then, composing her expression, she joined him.

The minute she sat down at the table he passed her a mug of coffee. Black and strong and sugarless, it was exactly how she liked it. 'Thank you,' she said devoutly.

Her relief was rapidly replaced by dismay at the plate he put in front of her, piled with more bacon than she normally saw in a year, as well as an egg and a tomato. And they were all, she realised with glum irritation, superbly cooked. 'You've used all my bacon. And I can't eat that much!' she objected.

'There's no fridge to keep food fresh, so the bacon has to be eaten today. Besides, you need it. You're going to have a busy day,' he said, bringing his own, much larger plate across.

Awed, Jan's glance went from his plate to hers. 'I am?' she asked weakly.

'Yes. I'll show you around the place, and then we'll go to the homestead so you can see I don't have a Bluebeard's tower there.'

Although there was amusement in his voice, there was also a calm purposefulness that told her he wasn't going to be gainsaid. Well, perhaps she'd let him act like the lord of the manor today. Then she could get on with her life and he could leave her alone. Resigned, she picked up her knife and fork and began to eat.

'Has anyone ever told you that you're bossy?' she asked politely after a while.

'Not since school,' he said. 'They usually use terms like autocratic, domineering or overbearing.'

'My mother brought me up to be courteous,' she explained.

'And succeeded magnificently.'

She gave him a sharp look, and met one of such blandness that it set her teeth on edge. Ignoring the open provocation in his tone, she retreated to a safe, if mortifying subject. 'I'd be very grateful if you'd show me how this place works. I did have a go at getting the range going yesterday, but all I got was smoke and resistance.' She had every normal person's acute aversion to eating humble pie and she had the feeling that it showed.

'Finish your breakfast first,' he said.

Amazingly, she did. Surveying the small heap of bacon rinds left on the edge of her plate, she said, 'We used to throw these to the seagulls when we were kids.'

'Thereby encouraging them to make a nuisance of themselves,' he said crisply. 'Don't feed them anything, and make sure you cover your rubbish bucket properly or you'll get rats.'

Repressing a shiver, she said, 'I suppose I bury the rubbish?'

'I'll collect it. Your grandfather gave it to us for pig food and compost. We gave him meat and vegetables in return.'

'He couldn't have produced much rubbish,' she said.

His broad shoulders moved in the slightest of shrugs. 'It was easier that way,' he said.

'What was he like?' As soon as she'd said the words she was astonished, but it was too late to recall them.

'Stubborn,' he said calmly. 'Intelligent.'

'Did he ever speak of—?'

'He was very reserved—he didn't have much time for people. Occasionally he'd talk about what was happening in the world, but usually he just greeted me and left it at that. He loved it here; he liked the solitude and the sea. He used to read a lot and he was a great walker.'

Had he deliberately kept an eye on the old man? Judging by his behaviour the night before, he could have. Kear Lannion appeared to have very patriarchal, protective attitudes towards women and old people. She should despise him for them, but something in her warmed at the thought of him making sure that her grandfather didn't live a completely solitary life. So she said, 'The solicitor told me he owned a hundred acres.'

'Most of it reverting to bush and some of it very steep. It would take a lot of money to bring it back in, and even then it wouldn't be an economic unit.'

Not if you wanted to farm it. But for what she had in mind, it was perfect.

Getting to her feet, she said, 'That was a brilliant meal. Thank you. I'll clear up.'

'I'll help.'

They worked in companionable silence, and when the few dishes had been washed in the bowl and dried, he showed her how to manipulate the levers in the range, so that the wetback heated water, and how to bank the firebox so that the fire wouldn't die. Like most things,

it was easy enough once you knew how. Then he revealed the mysteries of the spirit lamp, making her light
and douse it several times until she was reasonably
confident.

Apparently he was now reconciled to her staying in
the bach. All it had needed was a little firmness from
her, she told herself, trying to ignore the part of her mind
that was telling her he could probably give lessons in
determination. No doubt during the uncomfortable night
he'd decided he didn't really need this sort of hassle. It
wasn't as though she was important to him. In spite of
the previous night, they were strangers.

It was still before nine when they set off up the hill,
the Land Rover coping with the steep slope and gigantic
ruts much more easily than her little car had. But then,
like her, the MG was built for the city. Surveying the
kanuka trees with their spiky, scented little leaves and
ragged bark, Jan thought with astonishment that for the
first time in years she was happy—not for any reason
or because of something, but simply because she was
alive. As a child she used to wake each morning tasting
that keen, shining anticipation, so sharp it was hard to
bear; like many other childhood pleasures, the delight
had faded as she grew older. It was natural, but it seemed
sad.

'That's an enigmatic smile,' Kear observed lazily.

'I was just thinking there are lots of worse things to
be doing than driving through bush on a glorious autumn
morning, with the sea gleaming all the way to the
horizon.'

'Oh, there are indeed,' he said.

And I'll bet you've done some of them, she thought,
alerted by a raw note in his deep voice.

Hastily she said, 'It's unusual, surely, to have to cross
another person's land to get to a farm?'

'The county council, in its wisdom, decided to close
down your access road when the only other property on
it, a timber mill, went bankrupt. The councillors asked

my father if they could give your land access across Papanui. He agreed.'

'That was kind of him,' she murmured.

'First of all he made them seal the road to the entrance,' he drawled. 'And the raft of conditions he set up should have made the county think twice. Fergus had previously promised that if he ever wanted to sell he'd give us first refusal.'

Jan nodded. 'But he died without ever wanting to sell it.'

'Yes.'

Jan sent him a swift glance, but was baffled. There was nothing to be learned from that unyielding face. Anyway, the question of refusals didn't arise now. She wasn't going to sell. Opening her mouth to tell him, she closed it again before any impetuous word could escape. Not yet, she thought; she'd have to do some spadework before she made a final decision.

Straightening her shoulders, she pushed a vague unease to the back of her mind. 'Why is your farm called Papanui?'

'The area's been known by that name since soon after the first Maori arrived,' he said. 'It could mean a big plain, but as there's almost no flat land around here it's probably a reference to a sort of stage in a tree used as a seat by a bird-snarer. The story behind it's long forgotten.'

By then they had reached the fork where her road left his. He swung the Land Rover over the cattlestop. This time she noticed the difference between his green, smiling acres and the scrubby untidiness of hers.

'I thought we were going to have a look around my place,' she said.

He sent her that lethal, compelling smile. 'Do you mind if I go home and change first?'

Instant meltdown! If they could bottle that smile, Jan thought, striving for composure, he'd be the richest man in the world. Reluctantly, because she could imagine only too clearly how he must feel, she said shortly, 'No, of course not. Although if you hadn't been so stubborn you'd have spent the night in your own bed.'

'True,' he said. His mouth tilted slightly, as though he were remembering something.

Made uneasy, Jan said, 'Are you always so damned obstinate?'

'Are you?'

She shrugged. 'I resent being forced to do things,' she said, adding snidely, 'Especially sleeping with strange men.'

He didn't take her up on that not entirely felicitous comment. He merely said, 'We appear to suffer from the same complaint,' and turned the wheel so that they headed towards the peninsula where his house waited.

CHAPTER FOUR

JAN glanced at the bronzed forearms and strong, lean hands on the wheel. Try as she might to persuade herself that he was a stranger, she had achieved a much greater intimacy with this man than any other—she had even slept beside him. Slept, moreover, without stirring. Frowning at a shadowy memory, she looked out at four houses clustered quite close to each other in a valley that led down to the sea.

'The farm workers' cottages,' Kear said when she commented on them.

'Hardly cottages. And more workers than usual, surely?' she observed. Each substantial building was set behind neatly clipped hedges.

'The station is big, and a lot of it is steep. Mechanisation goes only so far.'

The road wound past stockyards, a woolshed and a variety of other sheds, all painted a khaki that harmonised with the grass.

'I like the way you haven't skinned your hills,' she said, working out what made his farm different. 'You've left the trees in the gullies. It looks much nicer.'

'Thank you,' he said, not trying to hide his amusement. 'It stops a lot of erosion too.'

'Those are pine plantations in some of the gullies, aren't they?'

'Pines and eucalypts. The timber is useful around the place and I sell any surplus. Prices are good for pine at present, and likely to get better. With the world shortage of timber, most farmers are planting woodlots where they can.'

The road skimmed the side of a hill before coming down again beside the sea. The homestead peninsula was bigger than she had realised—about the size of an average farm, she guessed, looking back at the area of cultivated land that stretched behind them. Papanui must be huge!

Ahead, the dark green domes of pohutukawa trees ringed the peninsular coast of coves and low cliffs, and backing a pinkish beach was a glorious seaside garden surrounding a large, double-storeyed mansion, handsomely conscious of the dignity of its eighty or ninety years.

'That,' Jan said on an outflow of breath, 'is a lovely house.'

Kear drove into a courtyard behind it, switched off the engine and said in the silence that rushed through the windows, 'It was built in the days when there were no roads. Guests came up in the scows that plied their trade up and down the coast, and they stayed until the scow came back.'

'I love Queen Anne houses,' Jan said, feasting her eyes on the bays and nooks that characterised the style. 'They have such character. Is there a ballroom?'

'Yes, as well as eight bedrooms, what used to be a library and is now a working office, four living rooms including the parlour, and servants' rooms above the kitchen wing.'

She sighed. 'Sheer hell to look after, but I do envy you the place. My mother would adore it.'

'You must invite her up to see it,' he said with cool courtesy, leaning across to open the door for her.

Jan jumped down and held out her hand to the black and white border collie that came officiously up to check her out. 'Who are you, then?' she asked.

'Sheba,' Kear told her. At the sound of her name, the dog left Jan and raced eagerly across to him. 'Good girl,' he said, and the dog gazed at him as though heaven had manifested itself.

In fact, Jan told herself, the look on Sheba's face bore a suspicious resemblance to the look most women seemed to wear when they looked at Kear. Even Gerry, who'd disguised flagrant interest with her air of street-smart worldliness, had lost some of her considerable cool whenever he'd smiled at her.

'I thought farm dogs were usually tied up,' Jan observed.

Kear said, 'My mother made a pet of her. She thinks she's the official greeter and watchdog. Come on in and meet my housekeeper.'

His housekeeper was a thin woman in her mid-forties, dressed in jeans and a white hip-length shirt, whom he introduced as Noelle Blair.

'Jan is Fergus Morrison's granddaughter,' he told her. 'While I'm getting changed would you make her some coffee?'

Noelle Blair, Jan realised with a startling stab of emotion, didn't seem in the least surprised that Kear had spent the night away. Perhaps he made a habit of it.

'I hope you didn't find Mr Morrison's place in too much of a mess,' Noelle said, bustling across the huge modernised kitchen to put on the coffee.

'It just needs a good cleaning,' Jan told her.

'I guessed it did when Kear rang this morning to say he'd collected you on his way home.' The housekeeper kept her expression well under control, but Jan recognised the glint of amusement for what it was. Like Kear, Noelle Blair thought she was a fish definitely out of water. Her next words reinforced Jan's conclusion. 'One of the men saw you arrive yesterday and Kear said he'd call in and see who was there. Are you going to stay here until it's tidied up?'

'No, I can manage,' Jan said placidly, looking around. 'What a magnificent kitchen. You could cook for an army in here.'

The housekeeper laughed. 'I have. Some years ago the military had a big exercise in the district, and as the man who ran it was a cousin of Kear's he spent a lot of time here with the foreign observers and dignitaries. It was a wild old week, believe me, but fun. And before Kear's parents went overseas we used to have weekend parties. Kear still does occasionally, but he doesn't have the time to entertain as much as his mother used to.'

She pulled out a cup and saucer and set them on a tray. 'So you're old Fergus's granddaughter. We didn't know he had any family.'

'I didn't know he was here,' Jan said without emphasis. 'We thought he was dead.'

After a shrewd glance the housekeeper nodded. 'These things happen in families,' she said.

She chatted on until the coffee was ready, mostly about the small happenings of a country district interspersed with a few polite questions, then picked up the tray and took Jan through to a room where a table dreamed in one of the bow windows.

'If you don't mind, I'll go on working,' she said. 'This house is like a sponge—it just soaks up time and effort.'

'I'm amazed that one woman can keep it under control.'

Noelle shrugged. 'I have help when I need it,' she said, then smiled at her again and left.

The coffee was excellent. Of course it would be; Kear wouldn't have it any other way. Jan looked out onto alien green hills beyond a glittering expanse of harbour, and tried to rid herself of the prickling fear that she had walked into something she didn't understand.

Kear Lannion had calmly taken over—staying with her last night, sleeping beside her. Yet she hadn't been shocked, or wary, or afraid, all of which would have been sensible responses to the situation. She'd accepted his assumption of authority with a bemused sense of inevitability and only a few token protests. In other words, she'd behaved with the spine of a jellyfish.

He'd cast a darkly ambiguous enchantment over her, she thought, setting down her cup with a sharp little click—a spell that subtly demolished the usual defences women erected when large, masterful and dangerously disturbing men strode into their lives. Well, she didn't need anyone looking after her, so after this tour of Papanui she'd make sure Kear understood that she ran her own life.

'Ah, there you are,' he said from the doorway. 'Ready?'

Cautiously Jan turned her head. Tall and commanding, the lean, whipcord strength now emphasised by a checked shirt and moleskin trousers, he should have looked bucolic, countrified—no threat at all. Instead, he exuded a worldliness that barely managed to leash his smouldering male sexuality. He had shaved, but that buccaneering look hadn't diminished; if anything, the removal of his beard emphasised the predatory angles of his jaw.

Shocked, Jan realised that she had been staring again. God, he'd think her a total idiot. She said with a briskness she hoped sounded authentic, 'Yes, thank you,' and picked up the tray.

In the kitchen he said, 'Oh, by the way, we'll be in for lunch, Noelle.'

'You're doing it again,' Jan said evenly when they were outside the room.

His brows lifted. 'Doing what?'

'Taking over.'

He looked at her as though she were gabbling some unknown language, then smiled, partly in irony and partly with a faint flash of some unknown quality that made her stomach muscles contract.

'Sorry,' he said on a note of mockery.

She said stiffly, 'I know I'm easy to overlook, but I don't like being treated like a halfwit.'

'Is that what I was doing?' he said. 'Odd, because I don't think you're easy to overlook at all. You stand out like a small but vivid bird of paradise. Are you going to have lunch with me?'

She had been going to refuse politely but firmly. Of course she had. Yet she said, 'Yes, thank you.'

'I'll show you around the house afterwards,' he promised, turning her with a light touch on her shoulder, then dropped his hand to her elbow as they walked down the wide, panelled hall to the back door. The barely noticeable pressure stretched her skin so taut that every tiny invisible hair stood up straight.

Deep inside the most primitive part of Jan's mind, something shrieked a warning. In a complex, unvoiced way she had conceded far more than a simple agreement to lunch. Yet it wasn't anger at her capitulation that possessed her. It was anticipation—heated, slow as a surrender and swift as the rush of victory, a powerful, radical jolt that rearranged her responses, her very thought processes, sizzling through logic and reason and common sense.

I can't control this, she thought starkly. I don't know what to do.

Still, after today she wouldn't be seeing much of him, she decided, taking comfort where she could. Clearly he felt some sort of obligation to her because she was a neighbour, but as soon as he realised she was capable of looking after herself he'd get over that. And if he didn't, she'd spell it out until he had to accept it.

Back in the Land Rover, he asked casually, 'How long do you plan to stay?'

She hesitated before saying, 'My grandfather wanted me to live here for a month. I don't know why.'

'Perhaps to establish some sort of connection,' he said, surprising her with his perceptiveness. 'So that he has some place in your mind.'

Yes, she could understand that. What she couldn't understand was why Fergus Morrison hadn't contacted her, at least when he'd come back to New Zealand.

Kear asked, 'How are you going to occupy your time?'

At her birthday party she'd tried to give him the impression that she'd go mad too far from shops and cafés. If his opinion mattered—which it didn't—she'd take great pleasure in showing him that she could cope with anything.

He flicked her a questioning glance. To her stunned chagrin she admitted, 'Actually, I want to write a book.'

'I see.' His voice was carefully neutral.

Defensively she said, 'I know there are some excellent books on the market for people who have difficulty choosing the right colours and style of clothes, but I've worked out a system that's unique and very simple to use. I have notes I've made over the years for seminars and talks and workshops, and I want to get them in some sort of order in case there's a book in there somewhere.'

'It sounds an excellent idea,' he said.

Sunlight transformed the auburn cast in his dark hair to a shimmering intensity of copper. Against the fresh autumn green of the paddock his profile was inscrutable and hard, a forceful combination of lines and angles broken only by the potently sensual curves of his mouth.

You're staring again, Jan hissed to herself, dragging her gaze away to fix it on the scenery outside.

He said, 'Do you work on a computer?'

'Yes, a laptop.'

'I see.' There was silence, until he asked, 'Just how were you planning to recharge it?'

'The usual— Oh, hell,' she said blankly, realising she'd just made a monumental fool of herself. Why hadn't Mr Gates warned her there was no electricity in the bach? Was this whole episode some sort of test she had to pass before she actually got her inheritance?

No, she was being paranoid, but she'd ring him when she got back to town and say something crisp and pertinent about sending her up here with no idea of what she faced.

If the corner of Kear's harshly beautiful mouth had moved, if he'd shown any sign of amusement at all, she'd have lost her temper.

'I didn't even think of it,' she said, expelling a long breath. 'What a twit!'

'You weren't to know there was no power in the bach. As for the computer—that's easily dealt with. I'll give you a room at the homestead as an office.'

Automatically she said, 'But I can't—'

'Why not?' His voice was maddeningly reasonable. 'I'm not there for most of the day, so you won't get in my way, if that's what's worrying you. The power you'll use won't show up on the bill in big red figures. And you'll be able to work.'

He was right, damn him. Jan chewed her lip, but knew she'd have to either accept his offer or find some way of getting power to the bach.

How stupid! She'd been so taken aback by the bach that she hadn't even thought of her jazzy little laptop, and then Kear had arrived and somehow taken over her brain. He should be forced to wear a notice, she thought angrily, knowing she was using him as a scapegoat— Danger! This man shreds your common sense, and probably your sanity too.

'That's very kind of you,' she said, hoping he couldn't hear the wary note in the words.

'But you hate being beholden,' he drawled. 'I don't blame you. If you like you can pay me rent.'

'Of course I will,' she said swiftly.

'Spoken like a true businesswoman. Now, look around. We're going up the side of the highest hill on Papanui. On the right you can see exactly where your grandfather's property is.'

Papanui's eastern boundary was the bush-covered hills that formed the southern head of Doubtless Bay, much higher than anything on the station itself. Kear's sunlit acres contrasted abruptly with her grandfather's land, on which neglect was revealed by the yellow hue of the grass, scrub creeping across the hills, and collapsing fences.

Protruding above the regenerating forest and from the pohutukawas along the coast were grey, dead limbs—

stark evidence of the ravages that the introduced possums wrought on native trees.

'It looks—forlorn,' she said as the Land Rover came to a halt beside a large concrete structure.

'He was happy,' he said calmly, switching off the engine.

Startled anew by his uncanny ability to read her mind, Jan got out of the vehicle and walked a few steps away to brood over the panorama. Sheba, who must have bounded onto the back of the vehicle before they'd set off, jumped down and frisked ingratiatingly towards her, tail wagging.

'Heel, Sheba,' Kear said sharply.

'I like dogs,' Jan told him, holding out her hand again. After giving it a perfunctory sniff Sheba took up her position close behind Kear. Jan looked around. From the concrete structure a smooth swathe of grass set off along the ridge. 'An airstrip,' she said. 'Is that a hangar?'

'No, it's the fertiliser store. If you look down over there you can see the bach.'

Sure enough, the little building stood squarely behind its bay. From here it looked romantically picturesque— the soft red roof against the green grass, a half-moon of beach, water gleaming sinuously through the khaki canopy of the mangrove swamp.

'Where's that?' Jan asked, pointing to a long sweep of sand to the north, backed by pohutukawa trees and a scattering of houses.

'Cooper's Beach. The peninsula you can see to the north-east is Karikari. Further north and well out of sight is Cape Reinga. Have you ever been there?'

She shook her head. 'No,' she admitted, feeling strangely sensitive about it.

'I'll take you up to Spirits Bay one day. Every New Zealander should go—preferably on a moonlit night when you can stand and watch the Tasman Sea and the Pacific Ocean meet, and listen for the spirits that go hand over hand down the line of the cliff to the last, loneliest pohutukawa tree in the world before leaving for their final journey to Hawai'iki.'

Something icy ran up her spine. 'It's one of the three great New Zealand places, isn't it?'

'The other two being?'

'Rotorua, of course, and Milford Sound. I've given seminars in both places.' She laughed. 'And if there were a hotel at Cape Reinga I'd have probably given seminars there too. But I'm glad there's not; some places should be left wild and unscathed.'

'If you can call a lighthouse and tourist buses unscathed,' he said ironically. His grey gaze was impersonal and oddly speculative on her face. 'I'll bet you're good at seminars. What exactly do you do?'

'All sorts. Workshops for people who want to dress well on a limited budget, and I also work with groups who feel inadequate in social situations. I talk to high school students and women in refuges. You'd probably be surprised at how many people go through life feeling utterly inadequate, and how often it begins with a conviction that they're ugly and stupid and badly dressed, and that there's nothing they can do about it. As for being good—I get asked back,' she said calmly.

She couldn't see Kear Lannion attending one. He was one of those rare creatures, a man who was completely sure of himself. He didn't have to worry about his image, or his attitude; he strode silently and purposefully through his life with uncompromising self-sufficiency. The only things that saved him from arrogance, she decided, were his intelligence and the insight revealed by his ability to read minds.

A wind eased in from the north, soft and warm with the scent of tropical seas on it, and teased the short strands of hair around her face. Attacked by baseless apprehension, she shivered.

'Hop into the Land Rover,' he ordered.

She obeyed. From the airstrip he took her along the excellent network of roads on Papanui, pointing out the boundaries of her land and, presumably without malice, giving her an excellent view of the gorse and manuka, ragwort and thistles, that encroached upon her land.

Jan discovered that he was a fascinating talker. Not that he dominated the conversation; in fact, after making him laugh with a recital of the disasters that had occurred at a motivational workshop she had given, she realised that he had managed to get her telling him far more about herself than she normally did.

That made her uneasily self-conscious. She didn't want to be so aware of him, to notice helplessly the way his voice remained cool and detached even when delivering the punchline to a very funny story. She didn't want to be impressed by his knowledge of a multitude of subjects, or respond to that heartbreaker of a smile, or the smooth, masculine grace of his movements.

And she certainly didn't want to be overwhelmed by his concentrated magnetism, because beneath it she sensed a harder, more primitively compelling Kear Lannion, with aspects to his character which he kept ruthlessly hidden.

A woman was walking along the road towards the last of the workers' cottages, a solid, compact woman, moving slowly with a baby on her hip and a bag in her hand. As the Land Rover slowed and stopped she turned with a pleased smile that evaporated when she saw Jan.

Jan scrambled out and the woman said, 'Oh, Kear—I—I'm sorry I'm late, but it's all right. I just have to give Liam his lunch at April's, and then I'll come on up. April says she doesn't mind having him in the afternoons 'cause he sleeps most of the time then. I thought—'

'I'd rather we stuck to our original arrangement that you work in the mornings. I told you to let me know if you're finding it too much,' he said, taking the baby and handing him over to Jan while he slung the bag into the Land Rover.

The woman—very young, Jan noted, barely in her twenties—said, 'It's not, it's not, really. I love working for you. I just slept in this morning—'

The baby in Jan's arms stretched up a chubby hand towards the tiny gold hoop in her ear. Sharply his mother said, 'Liam, no!'

'He's all right,' Jan told her, jiggling the warm, plump body effortlessly. She smiled into the little face. 'Aren't you, sweetie?'

'Where's your pushchair?' Kear asked harshly.

The woman said, 'It's broken.'

Kear's brows snapped together. Jan didn't blame the woman for flinching, or Liam's soft triangular mouth for drooping.

'How did that happen?' Kear asked, banishing the frown from his face and reaching out to ruffle the baby's hair.

The woman said, 'I did it.'

He looked at her, his gaze hard and deliberate. The younger woman said earnestly, 'Truly, Kear. I managed to squash it in April's car door. Everything's fine.'

Liam buried his face into Jan's shirt, and his mother said, 'Here, I'll take him. He'll mark your blouse.'

'It'll wash,' Jan said, but she handed the baby over. Smiling, she said, 'How do you do? I'm Jan Carruthers. I'm Fergus Morrison's granddaughter, and I'll be staying in his bach for the next month.'

'I'm sorry,' Kear said stiffly, 'I should have introduced you both. Jan, this is Tina Hopgood, who does my office work for me. Jump in the back, will you, so we can get going.'

As Jan did so she wondered at that slip in his excellent manners. Although he'd hidden it, he'd been angry. About what?

Tina settled herself and Liam in the front seat, then glanced at Kear before turning to Jan and saying, 'I know who you are, although you won't remember me. I went to a workshop you gave a few years back. At the Burnside Centre.'

'Did you?' Jan said, laughing a little. 'I hope you enjoyed it.'

'I wouldn't call it all enjoyable,' Tina said a little drily, 'but it was interesting.'

April was the wife of one of the farm workers, and looked after Liam with her own two small children for the four mornings a week that Tina worked at the homestead. After mother and child had been dropped off, Jan discovered that Tina was married to Brett, the station's mechanic.

'A nice girl,' Jan commented. Automatically, she corrected herself. 'Woman.'

'She's twenty,' he said. 'I considered myself a man at that age, but looking back I can see how far off the mark I was.'

'She's young to be married and with a baby.'

'Very.' His voice was flat and unemotional.

Jan's enquiring glance shattered on the remote, impervious line of his profile.

Something was definitely going on, she thought, and she had a horrid suspicion that she knew what it was.

She spent the rest of the drive trying very hard to convince herself that it was none of her business.

Back at the homestead a car waited; not a muscle changed in Kear's face as the Land Rover drew to a halt, but Jan thought she discerned a faint irritation in him.

'Friends,' he said calmly. 'Rod and Madeleine Harcourt. Rod farms inland.'

And also Madeleine's sister, Louise. Clearly, Kear liked rangy women; this one could have been a sister of the woman who had been with him at the polo match, and, although not as enchantingly lovely as Gerry, was the same physical type. They had come to deliver some papers, but were easily persuaded to stay to lunch.

Madeleine and Louise, Jan found out over an excellent meal, were women who'd made a vocation out of being a farmer's wife and sister-in-law. They talked knowledgeably of breeding cattle and they were clearly excellent hostesses, as well as being competent in everything that counted on a farm. They dressed in clothes of subdued good taste and obvious expense, chosen to look good and wear well rather than for fashion. Rod Harcourt was all bluff friendliness, but his wife, ably abetted by her sister, made it subtly obvious in ways that only another woman could understand that they considered Jan to be a frivolous, useless bimbo.

They also despised image consultants.

'Oh, one of the new professions,' Louise said, with an indulgent smile that didn't reach her eyes. 'Although I don't suppose it can be called a profession, really. It must be interesting.'

Squelching a defensive reply, Jan satisfied herself with a sweet smile and a non-committal comment. None of these people, and that included Kear, meant anything to her. Once she'd left Papanui she'd probably never see them again.

Although if her plans came to fruition it might be difficult to avoid Kear. Angrily, she realised that her main emotion at that prospect was a sneaky, forbidden pleasure.

Eventually it was time for the visitors to go. Feeling superfluous, Jan would have stayed behind to thank Noelle, but Kear took her elbow again—an automatic movement noted and resented by two pairs of feminine eyes—and kept her by his side.

'We can give you a lift back to Fergus's little shack,' Madeleine said. 'There's no need for Kear to waste time running you around when we're going past.'

'Thank—'

Kear interrupted blandly. 'That's kind of you, but Jan and I have a few things to discuss before I take her home.'

There were far too controlled to allow any irritation to appear, but Jan knew she was going to be a topic of conversation in that household.

When the car had left she said, 'What do we have to discuss?'

'The room I thought you might like to use as an office,' he said, looking down at her with slightly raised brows.

Something smouldered into life inside her. 'Oh, yes, of course,' she said, endeavouring to sound casual.

To reach the small room they had to go through the office. Tina, working at a computer, looked up and smiled as they came in. And who, Jan thought wearily, could blame her if her glance lingered on Kear?

'Through here,' Kear said, nodding at Tina. 'It used to hold files and ledgers. We keep them in a fire-proof vault now, along with the wine.'

The shelves on two walls had been removed, and beneath a window set high in the wall there was a bench on which she could put her computer.

'If this is too cramped,' he said, 'we can find you another room—one with a window you can actually see through.'

'One of the good things about being small is that rooms where other people get claustrophobia seem perfectly all right,' she told him. 'As for the window—if I had one that overlooked your wonderful gardens I'd be peering through it all the time instead of working.'

It was, she thought crossly, humiliating to be one of a long line of women who were knocked off their feet by that smile of his. Ah, well, if she worked things properly she'd not see much of him.

'Come up whenever you want to during the day,' he said.

'Thank you.' She walked with him through the office, smiled again at Tina, and said as they went out into the hallway, 'I'll head for home now, if that's all right with you.'

'Are you sure you wouldn't rather sleep here?' he said.

She said firmly, 'We've been through this conversation. I won't throw a wobbly just because a possum gets lovesick outside my window, and now I know how to use that range I'll be fine.'

He didn't try to persuade her to change her mind, for which she was grateful. Indeed, something about him had altered; he seemed to have withdrawn behind an armoured wall. Probably Madeleine and Louise's clever innuendoes about her had reached their target.

She didn't care, she thought on the way back to the bach. Not a bit.

He walked her to her door and said, 'I didn't have a chance to show you around the house.'

'Another time. Thanks for everything,' she said, finding to her astonishment that she had to strive for the small talk she usually took for granted.

'It was my pleasure,' he said aloofly.

Jan watched him go, then built up the range with some of the wood stacked against the side of the shed where her car was.

Some hours of hard work later she emptied yet another bucket of filthy water. Being able to heat it had made this battle with grime much easier than yesterday's. The walls no longer made her shudder, and, although the linoleum on the floors was cracked and hard to clean, she'd got most of the dirt off.

Except for the bedroom, which she'd do after she'd had a cup of tea, the inside of the bach had stopped looking like something one of Hollywood's best set designers had produced for a horror movie.

Cleaning house was better than going to the gym, Jan thought. And how fortunate that she did keep fit, because this really exercised those muscles!

Tomorrow, she decided a few minutes later, looking with dismay at the curdled milk and oily cheese sitting squalidly amongst the other food in the cupboards, she'd have to do some shopping. Living without a refrigerator was going to make a trip to the nearest store necessary at least every second day.

How had Fergus Morrison managed? Her grand-father hadn't sounded the most endearing of men but, apart from her mother, Anet and Great-Aunt Kit, he'd been her closest blood relative and she wished she'd known him. He might have told her more about her father, that handsome, reckless young man, who had killed himself driving too fast on a racetrack. Her mother spoke of Hugo Morrison with love and sympathy, but Jan knew little of his childhood.

With a cup of herbal tea in her hand, Jan stood in the doorway, wrinkling her nose at the combination of the faint, muddy smell of the mangrove swamp overlaid by an unknown sweetness, pervasive and strong, and wondering just what particular form of life caused the sharp cracking noises that occurred whenever the tide was out. Crabs? Some sort of bird? Kear would know.

She needed to explore the bay thoroughly, but she was almost certain it would suit her plans. Not that she de-luded herself that it would be easy—somehow the few dedicated fundraisers for the centre would have to find the large amount of money needed for such boring and expensive but necessary systems as drainage and elec-tricity, as well as for buildings. She could, of course, ask her stepfather, and no doubt he'd help her, but he had his own charities.

It would all take so much time! There was the whole procedure with the Resource Management Act to go through, and that would mean persuading the locals that the adolescents who came here would not run amok around the district.

Images of Kear's strong face loomed forebodingly as she wondered just what he would say to a camp for 'wayward girls' being set up on his doorstep.

Oh, well, she'd cross those bridges when she came to them.

After their quick drive around, she could see why he wanted to buy her land. He had shown her the weeds that continually invaded his property from hers—as well as gorse and ragwort and the thick thatch of dead thistles, there were gums and wattles and tobago weed all encroaching through the fence lines—and he'd told her casually how much he spent on weedkillers each year, a sum that had made her blench.

Although people might give money to build dormitories and put in plumbing for a camp, they would not see the necessity to use any of it to kill weeds. Yet it certainly wasn't fair that Kear should have to deal with what was essentially her problem. And she should, she thought guiltily, have told him that she had no intention of selling her unexpected inheritance to him.

Which brought up an even more uncomfortable thought. Why hadn't she?

Surely not because she didn't want them arrayed on opposing sides just yet?

Appalled by the idea, she quickly found another to replace it. If she wrote and sold this book it might bring in enough to set up a trust fund for the centre.

And if that didn't work, she thought suddenly, she could always sell the miniature.

She went into the bedroom and fossicked through the drawer in the wardrobe. Of course the suede bag was at the bottom, lying confidingly in between a bra and a pair of briefs. Opening the drawstring, she pulled out the miniature, then took it outside into the sunlight so that she could see it properly.

The exquisite features looked firm and slightly arrogant, the dark brows straight and determined. Anet had said it would be all right to pass her on, she thought, running a light caressing finger around the wooden frame. Would selling it be construed as handing it on?

Her head full of plans, Jan smiled at the enchantingly aristocratic face.

'You remind me of someone,' she said, half laughing at the foolishness of her thoughts. 'Someone who lives not very far from here. It's that serene confidence. And now that I come to think of it, you and he have exactly the same eyebrows! You're not a relative, by any chance?'

As though her words had summoned Kear, the Land Rover came down the hill. Jan fought down the anticipation that licked through her veins as she waited for him.

'I forgot to tell you—' he began, then asked sharply, 'What's that?'

He was looking at the miniature.

'It's my birthday present from my sister,' she said. 'Lovely, isn't she? I'll bet she was a handful.'

'May I see?'

She handed the precious thing over, smiling as she saw the care with which he handled it, the long fingers that had pulled her away from the horse with such brutal strength curving gently around the frame. With an expressionless face he scrutinised the portrait, hard eyes remote behind the thick screen of his lashes.

For some reason a slow nervousness robbed her of wits. As Sheba sat beside him, head on one side, Jan searched the angular bronzed features, wondering just what was going on in his mind.

'Beautiful,' he said at last, handing the miniature back. His brows were drawn straight, and when she looked up it was to meet narrowed, oblique eyes.

While she'd been working great puffy white clouds had arrived from the same direction as the sun, but although some had carried the threat of rain they'd departed without releasing any of it. Another one passed over them now, moving swiftly, chilling Jan with its sudden, dark shadow.

'Where did you say you got it?' Kear asked absently.

'My sister Anet gave it to me for my birthday,' she repeated.

His gaze remained watchful, almost measuring. 'She has excellent taste,' he said. 'I gather it isn't a family heirloom?'

Jan's fingers curled protectively around the little portrait. 'No,' she said. 'It was given to Anet by friends of ours, Olivia and Drake Arundell. Apparently there's some sort of history to it—Anet said in her letter she'd tell me about it, but it sounds as though you have her for only a short time and then pass her on. I don't know who painted it, or who the subject is.' She curbed her runaway tongue and finished lightly, 'She has great style, hasn't she? One of Anet's better birthday presents. And I'd better take her inside before the sun burns her pretty face.'

'You've cut your finger,' Kear said suddenly as she put the portrait in its protective bag.

'I caught it on a nail. I've been cleaning.'

He picked up her hand and turned it over so that he could examine the small tear in her skin. His brows drew together.

How long did they stand there, her hand curled in his fingers, his thumb moving slowly over the faint blue veins in her wrist? For the space of three heartbeats, perhaps, before she pulled away and said offhandedly, 'It'll be all right. I just took off my gloves to do something and caught it. I never infect.'

He said roughly, 'I came to tell you that Noelle can give you a day's work—'

'That's very kind of her, but it's good for me,' she returned, moving away. 'Excellent exercise.'

Heartbeats still hammering in her ears, she led the way into the bach.

CHAPTER FIVE

INSIDE Kear looked around and said half angrily, 'You must be exhausted.'

Jan replied, 'Far from it. I might look fragile and useless, but I have reasonably sturdy muscles.'

'So I see,' he said, his tone as enigmatic as the expression on his face. 'A woman of constant surprises. Beautiful yet hard-working.'

'The two quite often do go together,' she observed tartly. 'Only unintelligent people think in stereotypes. I mean, I could look at you and come up with the classic romantic cliché—tall, dark, handsome and loaded. It's rather offensive, isn't it?'

Deep in those translucent grey eyes some warning flared, and the smile he gave her was ambiguous enough to be a threat. However, when he spoke his voice was cool and level. 'Point taken. I'm not romantic, as it happens.'

'Neither,' she said, 'am I.'

It was a challenge of sorts, although she didn't know why she should fling the words quite so staunchly at him.

Controlling the watchful intensity of his eyes and his tone, he said, 'Perhaps one day we should drink a toast to calm reason.'

'Speaking of which,' she said, glad to change the subject, 'I have a problem with food. Nothing's going to keep without a fridge so I'll have to go into the village every other day, but there's nowhere to keep it when I buy it. I'd have thought my grandfather would have had some sort of pantry.'

His brows drew together. 'There used to be a safe,' he said. 'It's not as efficient as a fridge, but it would at least give you a place to keep things.'

They found it, a cupboard with wire mesh on all four sides, hanging from a hook in the branch of one of the pohutukawa trees that clung to the headland. A year had thoroughly grimed it.

'I'll clean it now,' Jan said.

He lifted the safe off the hook. 'You'd better leave any groceries that need refrigeration at the homestead. We have a chiller room, so there's plenty of space. That way you won't have to go into the village so often.'

'You're too kind,' she said automatically. 'But it will do me good to get out.'

'You sound as though this place is a prison.'

'I didn't mean to.' But she had.

That equivocal smile returned, but all he said was, 'I'm going in myself tomorrow morning at ten, so I'll pick you up on my way past.'

'OK.' He was taking over again. She should mind; unfortunately, she didn't. 'Actually, if it's all right with you, I'll meet you at the homestead. I checked the computer and somehow I've managed to run it right down, so it can be recharging while we're away. Oh, I meant to ask you before—I hammered the sides of the tank with a stick, and I can tell how far down the water is, but how long is it going to last?'

'That depends entirely on how much you use,' he said maddeningly, putting the safe down on the grass. He caught her baffled frown and gave a sudden grin.

Jan watched him straighten up, amazed at the sudden wild gyration her heart performed in her chest. He moved with such economy, she thought, trying to find the right words to describe him, as though by doing so she could lessen the impact he made on her, pin down the inchoate, transient experience like fastening butterflies to a board. She wanted her feelings as neatly catalogued, as easy to control.

'It's full to two rungs from the top,' she said thinly, going to get the scrubbing brush she'd put out in the sun to dry.

'You haven't used much,' he said, and looked up into the sky. 'It will almost certainly rain tonight, so you'll be right. At this time of the year you won't run out if you're reasonably economical with showers and baths. Summer is an entirely different story.'

'Thanks,' she said.

'Here, give me that brush.'

She clutched it. 'Kear, I'm perfectly capable of scrubbing out a safe!'

His smile didn't reach his eyes. 'Of course you are,' he said, a note of derisory amusement in his voice. 'You've convinced me you're as tough as overcooked steak, but somehow my eyes don't believe it.'

'You'll get used to it,' she consoled him.

The lazy irony in his smile seemed directed more at himself than her, but it left a lingering disquiet that stayed with her for the rest of the day.

His attitude was one she'd come across often. Most men—and, infuriatingly, too many women—took one look at her and decided she was a weak, ineffectual piece of fluff with nothing to offer but slanted blue eyes and a pretty face. Usually it didn't take long to convince them otherwise, but she'd had to fight some battles over the years.

Men like Kear Lannion, who used their strength to protect, could be the worst offenders, along with those men whose egos needed the reassurance of a woman they could dominate physically. Over the years she'd learned to differentiate between them.

Picking up her trusty rubber gloves, she began on the safe. Fortunately the interior had been painted in some glossy paint, so the dirt was only superficial, but for hygiene's sake she scrubbed it twice.

All this manual work, she thought when the safe was drying in the sun, gave her time to think. And if she wasn't to fret about Kear and his effect on her, she'd better fasten onto another subject.

By the time she'd scrubbed halfway up the first wall in the bedroom she'd found one. Tina Hopgood, who had been to one of her workshops. Well, that wasn't so unusual; over the years several hundred girls had done the same. And it wasn't surprising that she hadn't recognised the girl either. She just wished she didn't have this uneasy feeling that all was not right with her. Ludicrous it might be, but she couldn't banish a lingering feeling of responsibility.

The sun was behind the hills to the west when at last she bathed and washed her hair and made a list of shopping necessities. By the time she'd finished, the evening was drawing in. Hastily, before the mosquitoes roared out in their bloodthirsty squadrons, she closed the windows and lit the lamp, sighing with satisfaction when it was done. Tomorrow, she decided, gazing around a bedroom as clean as modern detergents, elbow grease and determination could make it, she'd finish this scrubbing marathon.

Too tired to cook a meal, she made herself a salad sandwich, rang Kear—who wasn't there—chatted with Noelle for a few minutes and read for an hour or so before going to bed. This time when the possums chattered outside she surfaced for a startled moment, then immediately turned over and went back to sleep.

Although the night was as warm as the previous one, she woke with a faint, lingering chill. However, morning welcomed her with a clear sky and the generous warmth of a sun not ready to admit that it was autumn.

'I could get used to this,' she murmured as she sat at the table with her coffee and watched the shags on the dead white branches of an old tree stretch out their wings to dry.

'Don't,' she warned herself, getting up with a wry little smile. 'This is not your life.'

By nine-thirty the last of the cleaning was done and she was donning a skirt and light shirt. Settling for no more make-up than a touch of lipstick, she applied it and then tidied her hair. Uncompromisingly cut in an urchin style, the feathery fronds set off her small, neat features, and it was blissfully easy to look after.

She set the comb down and turned away from the mirror, resisting the slow, sensuous tide of excitement that rose through her, inexorable, frightening.

If she'd been ten years younger she might have thought she was falling in love, but she knew love didn't come helter-skelter after a few meetings. It grew gradually, like all things that lasted and were solid. No, what she felt for Kear was chemistry, the desire of the eye, a hidden, atavistic compulsion to reproduce. She had looked at Kear and for some reason she had wanted him.

Cynically, she thought that if she made her feelings obvious he'd probably sleep with her. Many men didn't seem to be particularly fussy about who they went to bed with. Was Kear like that? No, she suspected that he was innately fastidious. But he was experienced. A woman could always read the subliminal signals that indicated a man who knew how to pleasure his lovers. Something in the way he moved, perhaps, gave away the secret—that casual, lethal grace, the authoritative air of self-control.

This, she told herself sternly, is not getting you anywhere. The thing to remember was that she was definitely not in the market for a casual affair.

If she couldn't have the sort of love Anet had found with Lucas, and their friend Olivia with her husband Drake, she'd go without. Passion was a weak, unsatisfactory substitute, like eating dry husks instead of good food.

'Only a month,' she said aloud.

All this was academic anyway. If, as she suspected, Kear was attracted to her, he certainly wasn't doing anything about it beyond being neighbourly.

She shrugged and pulled the latch on the door. Even that first night, when he'd insisted on sleeping beside her, he'd been what Cynthia would describe as a 'perfect gentleman.'

Yet that wasn't how he came across. In spite of his disciplined restraint, danger swirled about him in an unseen aura, a kind of glamorous peril that made her understand why some women fell in love with the wrong men.

She got into the MG and drove gingerly, the laptop belted in beside her, up the track between the leggy, feathery kanuka trees. She hadn't noticed before that just to one side a stream kept pace with the track, dropping down towards the sea in a thicker cloak of native bush. She'd explore there some time, she promised herself.

Kear came riding in as she arrived at the homestead, smiling at her before swinging off his horse with the casual expertise of a man who didn't have to think about what he was doing. Instead of jodhpurs he was wearing boots and well-cut trousers, a dark shirt that showed off the width of his shoulders, and a low-crowned hat.

Horses were strange animals, Jan thought, watching him remove the bridle and saddle with deft, easy movements. They had the power to ennoble their riders, to turn them into demigods. It was probably a hangover from the days when humans had been thrilled and awe-struck by their newfound ability to tame horses. The animals might have been relegated to mere utility over the centuries, but about them still hung some remnants of that primal mystery.

'Give me ten minutes,' Kear said after he'd greeted her. 'Noelle will make you some coffee.'

And he was gone before she could protest. She took the computer into her office, plugged it in and patted it gently, then refused coffee in favour of exploring the closest part of the garden. Occasionally she stole a glance at the house. Which was Kear's bedroom?

She saw no movement behind the curtains, but within the ten minutes he appeared at the long French windows

of the dining room, clad this time in casually elegant
trousers and a short-sleeved shirt of fine cotton, and said,
'Sorry about that. I had a minor emergency to deal with.'

'All well?'

'Yes.' He didn't say any more and she didn't ask, contented to walk beside him down a path where shells
scrunched pleasantly underfoot, smelling the scent of
white bouvardia, its long tubular flowers and scent
lending a sentimental, old-fashioned air to the garden.

'We'll take my car, I think,' he said, eyeing hers as
he opened the gate onto the parking area outside the
garden. 'I doubt whether I can fit my legs in yours.'

He drove a large, fairly new car, a gleaming monster
that coped, he said, with northern roads.

The business he had in the village consisted of five
minutes at the local bank. The rest of the time he spent
with her, making sure that the owners of the various
shops knew who she was. He took her into the Post
Office, where she found three coconut-palm-scattered
postcards from her mother in Fiji and a letter from a
friend. Tucking them into her bag for later reading, she
then accompanied Kear to the store that squatted on piles
over the waters of the harbour. To her delight Jan discovered that if she peered through the knotholes in the
planked floor she could see waves sluicing beneath.

Feeling absurdly conspicuous, she was introduced to
the owners and made welcome. It was interesting to note
the unspoken, far from servile yet very real respect that
Kear elicited from his neighbours.

'Thank you,' she said as she got back into the car.

'For what?'

'Showing me around,' she replied, not trying to
conceal the hint of dryness in her tone.

'It's nothing,' he told her, smiling at her with lazy,
coercive charm.

She said slowly, 'I get the feeling I've just been tucked
under a rather powerful wing.'

His eyes gleamed with mockery. 'I know it's no longer politically correct, but then we're a bit behindhand in the country.'

'Don't give me that,' she retorted. 'You're as sophisticated as any man I know. I wish I was six inches taller and didn't look like some little doll.'

But her words lacked bite.

'No doll I've ever seen has had eyes like some slumbrous Oriental beauty or a mouth soft with delicious, decadent promises,' he said coolly. 'You certainly don't remind me of a doll. A slightly wicked, provocative sprite from the green hills, perhaps—the sort young men were warned to avoid in case they lost their souls.'

Glowering down at her hands, Jan noted that they were clasped tightly together. 'Thank you,' she said in a deadpan voice. 'I thought you said you weren't a romantic.'

'I don't think sprites were romantic,' he said casually. 'Not in the way we use the word. They were dangerous, irresistible, perilous forces of nature, with all the shocking beauty and indifference that the term implies.'

'But only a romantic man would think of comparing me to such a thing,' she said, wondering why she didn't just shut up.

'I come of Cornish stock. We have some intriguing family legends about the kind of faerie you remind me of,' he said, his voice ironic.

She didn't know how to deal with that, so she said vaguely, 'How fascinating,' and then determinedly banished the subject. 'I really am quite competent to run my life, you know, but it was a nice gesture.'

'Think nothing of it,' he said negligently.

Those translucent eyes, glimmering like starshine, couldn't really be called opaque, yet it was impossible to see beyond that surface sheen. Baffled and acutely self-conscious, Jan listened as he began to talk of the impact of tourism on the north, and the change from farming to forestry.

When he wasn't teasing her about sprites and faeries he was more interesting than any other man, she thought, and realised even as she thought it that she was slipping faster and faster into unknown, hostile territory.

At the homestead they were met by one of his men, who said, 'God, I'm glad you're back. I was just going to see if Max was at home.'

'What's happened?'

The man pushed his hat onto the back of his head. 'Well, it's young Brett—'

'What's he done now?'

'Ah, well, he's put the 'dozer in Sandy Bay Creek. Not the big one—'

'Is he all right?' The question came hard and fast.

'Well, yeah, he's OK—that is, I thought he'd broken an arm, but he can move it so I suppose it's all right— but the 'dozer looks pretty sick. It's stuck, and I—'

'Start at the beginning and tell me exactly what happened.'

Jan noted with interest the way Kear elicited explanations from someone who tended to wander from the subject. Each time the farm worker began to stray Kear inserted an incisive question that got him back on track, and without being rude or flustering him.

After the tale was told he was silent for a few seconds, then he turned to Jan. 'I'm sorry, I have to go.'

'Of course you do. Thank you for taking me into the village.'

Kear had persuaded her to leave her spare milk and butter and cheese in the chiller room, so she walked into the homestead with the bag and tracked Noelle down. The housekeeper was bringing a bucket of pears into the kitchen.

'We've got a tree out in the garden that's older than the house,' she explained as Jan helped her put them onto a wire rack in the vegetable pantry. 'I bottle them with preserved ginger. Kear likes them for his breakfast sometimes. How about a coffee now?'

As they waited for the coffee to brew Jan mentioned the bulldozer accident.

'He'll be all right,' Noelle said. 'You couldn't kill Brett.' She frowned and said slowly, 'Tina's my niece. She tells me she went to some sort of seminar you gave.'

'Yes, so I believe.'

Noelle reached up into the cupboard that held the mugs. With her back to Jan she said, 'Apparently it was after she'd heard you talk that she decided to come up here, get away from the crowd she was running with in Auckland. I'd suggested she come up here before—Kear was quite happy for her to help me here—but until you made her think about where she was going, told her that she had no self-esteem and that she could get it if she worked, she hadn't wanted to come. She says you gave her the impetus to make a new life for herself.'

'It looks as though she's done that,' Jan said tentatively.

Noelle set the mugs down with a fierce little click. 'She met Brett.'

Silently Jan waited.

'Children having children, I say,' Noelle said angrily. 'And although there are some who make good little mothers—and, give her credit, she does try—it's only natural to feel trapped.'

While Jan was disentangling this Noelle poured the coffee and sat down. 'And that family of Brett's—well, if I'd had a daughter I wouldn't have wanted her to marry a Hopgood,' she said almost to herself.

Jan tried to look interested but not avid.

Noelle added milk to her mug. 'Kear's keeping an eye on them. The problem is...' Her voice trailed away and she said in a surprised tone, 'You're easy to talk to.'

'I'm not a counsellor, but I've done several papers and you learn a lot just by being at the centre.'

'I suppose so.' Noelle was clearly rearranging her thoughts.

'She seems lonely,' Jan said.

'She's quite friendly with April Pearson, and she talks to me when she comes up here, but she thinks I'm old and past it.'

Choosing her words carefully, Jan asked, 'Do you think Tina is being abused?'

'Not now. Well, as far as I know she's not. He was hitting her, but Kear found out and tore strips off him. He threatened him with jail and said he'd ring the police if Brett didn't go on an anger-management course. And he's sent him into the single men's quarters until Tina is ready to take him back. Kear made it more than clear that if he put a foot wrong he was in deep trouble.'

Jan nodded. 'So what's the problem?'

Noelle looked uncomfortable. 'She said yesterday that Brett wants them to get back together again.'

'And she doesn't want it?'

Noelle snorted. 'She didn't while she had a crush on Kear, but I think she's over that now. She's started saying she's lonely, and that Liam needs his father. And she's finding it hard looking after him and working in the office here and keeping up with her housework.'

'So you think she might give in.'

'Brett wants her to go away with him—says he's got a better job. He's promised her he won't ever hurt her again. She seems to believe him.'

'And you don't?' Jan said quietly.

'I'd be a lot happier about it if his father didn't beat his mother. I think Tina wants to believe him. But if they leave here, who's to know?'

Jan nodded.

'I don't know what to do,' Noelle said heavily.

'The only thing you can do,' Jan told her, 'is let her know that you'll always be here for her.'

'If she doesn't know that by now, she's been living in dreamland,' Noelle said.

'Tell her,' Jan insisted gently.

Eventually she got to her computer—more than half-charged, she noted with pleasure—and had been working for some time when she heard someone moving around next door. A couple of hours of concentrated work later she went through into the office and found Tina sitting at Kear's state-of-the-art computer, frowning at the screen.

'Hi,' she said. 'How are you?'

Tina jumped, and gave her a startled glance. 'I'm fine.' She paused, then asked deliberately, 'Did you enjoy your trip with Kear?'

'Yes, I did, thank you.'

Tina had large brown eyes. She kept them fixed on Jan as she asked, 'Are you Kear's latest girlfriend?'

'No,' Jan told her cheerfully.

'You like him, though, don't you?'

'He's been very good to me,' Jan replied noncommittally. 'Yes, I like him. Do you?'

Tina said, 'He's been very good to me too.'

'Is your husband all right?'

Tina flushed. 'Oh, yeah. Max—he's the manager—wanted to take him in to the doctor, but Brett says there's nothing wrong with him—he's just bruised his arm. He'll be all right.'

The hard, hopeless note embedded in the young voice made Jan wince. She had heard it before, often, and knew what it represented. Keeping her tone casual, she said, 'I imagine life's pretty tiring for you with young Liam.'

Tina shrugged. 'You get used to it,' she said defensively. Her gaze wandered to the screen of the computer, then flicked back to Jan. She said, 'Women chase Kear all the time.'

To which there seemed no logical answer. Jan said, 'Poor man,' in as sympathetic a voice as she could manage.

'Miss Carruthers?' Tina began almost truculently.

Jan said, 'Yes?'

The younger woman stared at her with eyes that saw past her, then said, 'Oh, nothing,' and began to type again.

One of the most difficult things Jan had been forced to accept over the years was that there was no easy answer, no simple cure for the many and various kinds of pain humans inflicted on themselves and each other.

Yet instances of the human spirit triumphing over appalling abuse were not rare either.

Determinedly, she recalled some of those instances as she drove back to the bach. Once there, she left the computer inside and walked onto the soft pale sand of the beach. Purple cloud shadows raced each other across the silver-blue water and the dark olive-green of the bush on the hills, only to be driven off by the mellow sunlight of autumn. The air was crisp and fresh, tanged with salt and the infinitely satisfying scent of growing things.

'If there's any way I can do it,' she said out loud, 'I'm going to turn this into a place of healing.'

She hung the safe back on the hook in the curved, massive branch of the pohutukawa tree, then checked it for any tears in the wire mesh. No, not even the most determined fly would be able to wriggle through. Ants, however, were another story. She decanted food into the containers she'd bought at the store and carried them out. It was certainly much cooler in the heavy shade of the tree than in the bach.

The range needed a couple of small logs delivered to the firebox before she made herself a sandwich. Tomorrow, she thought, when she went to write at the homestead, she'd see if she could get Tina to talk to her. Of course there were always cases that no one could help. If self-esteem was too low...

The next morning dawned cloudy and dull. It had rained in the night and would rain again, Jan thought, picturing grey curtains of moisture slanting across the bay, hiding the mangroves. It had been a most unusual season, with the temperatures staying higher for much longer than they normally did.

She went out to check the road, eyeing the ruts suspiciously. Her car was not accustomed to such roads, and neither, she admitted reluctantly, was she. Although the sun was drying the surface quickly, she decided that a walk would do her good; it couldn't be more than a couple of kilometres to the homestead.

Almost halfway there she met an extremely large tractor, bright green and yellow in colour, trailing a complicated piece of machinery that seemed all teeth and claws. Jan moved smartly onto the grass; a careless masculine hand waved from inside the cab and she glimpsed a young, good-looking face as the rig roared past.

Brett, Tina's husband, who had put the bulldozer in the creek? If so, he didn't look like a wife-beater. Jan's mouth pulled into an ironic smile. Not many wife-beaters did.

Noelle met her at the homestead. 'Kear's had to go out,' she said. 'He'll be back about mid-morning. Come on in; it looks as though you've brought the rain with you.'

'Do you need it?'

The housekeeper laughed. 'Not today. Not even this week. In fact, when that first shower came at ten last night Kear was saying that in all the years they've kept records here there's never been a season like it; we've got more grass and hay and silage than ever before.'

Today no brown-eyed secretary sat in the office. Switching on her computer, Jan set to work, drawing up possible chapter plans, grouping subjects, trying to rank her material systematically. She no longer felt a fraud; back at the bach the previous afternoon she'd continued to work at her laptop until it had informed her loftily that as she'd used up all the battery it was going to sleep.

She'd work out a way of organising her notes. Once the material was in some sort of order she'd have a much better idea of whether there was a book hidden in there or not. She rather suspected there was.

Lost in her work, she gave a startled glance over her shoulder when Kear said her name from the doorway. 'Oh, hello,' she muttered, pressing the keys that would save everything she'd done so far.

'How's it going?'

She swivelled around. The wonderful, comforting, stimulating scent of coffee wafted across her nostrils. 'Hard,' she admitted. 'I didn't realise it was going to be so difficult.'

'Not such a good idea, perhaps?'

She frowned. 'I won't know until I get it done.'

'But if it doesn't gel you'll have wasted a lot of time.'

She looked affronted. 'Who says it'll be wasted? I'll have learnt something. And if you don't want to get trampled in the rush, you'd better get out of the way. I can smell coffee.'

Laughing, he stood to one side. 'In my office, on the table in the window.'

His office was a huge room, almost as big as the drawing room, with panelled walls and bookshelves, a splendid oriental rug glowing in rich, dark mystery on the floor and two paintings from his collection on the walls. Jan had liked the room instantly, and found her pleasure in it increasing every time she went in.

He had set a tray on a table between a sofa and two armchairs that stood in a pool of sunlight in the big window. Late golden roses irradiated a dark green glass vase, holding all the warmth and serenity of autumn in their apricot and amber hearts.

'Mmm, glorious,' she said, bending to smell them.

'Better than coffee?'

She directed a slanted sideways glance up through her lashes. 'As good,' she admitted, straightening up and feeling foolish. That had been provocative—a flirtatious gesture she should have quelled.

His brows were raised slightly, but all he said was, 'I thought you were an addict.'

'My mother thinks I am, but you know mothers. I really only drink it in the morning.' She sat down, and at his invitation lifted the heavy silver pot and poured him a cup.

'My mother says,' he observed, 'that the Victorians knew something when they made such ornate tea and coffee-sets.'

Jan looked at him enquiringly, then wished she hadn't. A glint in the glacial eyes sent a swift, convulsive surge of sensation through her. Almost breathlessly she asked, 'What did they know?'

'Just how delicate those heavily decorated pots made every woman's wrists seem as she poured from them.'

With a snort, Jan filled a cup for herself. 'I can think of several unpleasant names to call anyone who thinks fragility is sexy,' she said.

'My mother got in before you.'

Something unusual happened to the base of her spine. Unfortunately it wasn't confined to that area; like a tide of velvet it flowed through her, stroking her nerves with seductive languor. 'I think I'd like your mother,' she said crisply.

'Yes, I think you would. She'd like you too.'

Flattered, and a little flustered, Jan picked up her coffee-cup. This intelligent, complex man fascinated her. Why had he grown up feeling responsible for everyone he met?

'Does she live here?' she asked.

'No. My father's health isn't good. Humidity is particularly trying for him so they live in Australia for four months of each year, the South of France for another four, and four in Colorado in America.'

She looked surprised. 'Do they enjoy such a nomadic life?'

'I think my mother would prefer to settle down, but they have friends everywhere they go and my father is the centre of her world.'

She nodded.

'No feminist retort?' he quizzed.

Jan's shoulders moved. 'Health is not exactly something you can compromise about, and I've never met a feminist who says you aren't allowed to love your husband, or make sacrifices. Provided, of course, that they're freely made. Do you have problems with uppity women?'

'No,' he said, 'I find them stimulating.'

The word dropped into the quiet room like a small bombshell. Jan didn't quite know why it shocked her so much, but it took all her professional composure to say lightly, 'Then aren't you glad you live nowadays, when there are so many about!'

His smile was watchful and narrow, his eyes glinting beneath the curly sweep of lashes which should, she thought confusedly, soften the ruthless dynamism of his face. However, they failed entirely—as did the severe, sculptured beauty of his mouth.

'They've always been around,' he said drily. 'Sometimes they've had to lie low, but they were there. My father certainly didn't have any difficulty finding my mother.'

Jan appeased a small portion of her consuming curiosity by asking, 'Do you look like either of them?'

'I have the Lannion stamp. If you're interested I'll show you the family portraits one day.'

Easing back into her chair, she drank more coffee before saying, 'I'd like to see them. You said you came of Cornish stock. How long have your family been here?'

'A hundred years, give or take a few.'

She wondered whether to go on with her gentle inquisition. He didn't look forbidding, or even remote, so she ventured, 'Do you have any brothers and sisters?'

'A brother, a couple of years younger than I am, who's a professional polo player. He's in Argentina at the moment,' he said without expression.

'Oh.' Since the day she'd decided that her blush clashed with the colour of her hair, Jan had trained herself to stay cool; she'd carried off some appalling moments without any change to the colour of her skin. But now, to her horror, a tell-tale heat flooded up from her breasts and swamped her skin. She ignored it. 'I never did find out,' she said, 'whether your team won or not that day.'

'We did.'

'Good for you,' she said. 'Did I ever thank you for rescuing me?'

He put his cup down on the table. Lord, she thought, as she did so often, but he was big. Why did it affect her so? For some reason she found Kear overwhelming—a threat all the more hazardous because he'd been kind to her.

He said now, 'Yes, you did. Would you like to tell me just what you were doing in that ridiculous outfit?'

After she'd explained he said austerely, 'You could have been killed.'

'I know,' she said with a slight shiver. 'Gerry was horrified. So was I. We should have made sure the hat was firmly attached.'

'It would have been sensible,' he agreed.

There was no censure in his voice, but she felt a total idiot. 'Well, we learned our lesson. It won't happen again.'

'Do you model much?'

'No, I'm too short. They want long-stemmed women in the modelling world.'

The sound of a large piece of machinery starting up some distance away reminded her of something. She said tentatively, 'Was that Tina's husband I met this morning, driving a huge green and yellow tractor with a science fiction piece of machinery on behind?'

The signs of his withdrawal were subtle but, to Jan's quick eye, unmistakable. 'A tedder,' he said, not smiling. 'Yes, that was Brett.'

And before she had a chance to speak he began to talk of something else.

Being a good guest, she followed suit, but when she arrived back at the bach she wondered at his response. He'd probably thought she was being nosy, she decided.

Trying unsuccessfully to drive his image from her mind, she made herself an egg salad. As she ate the cloud mass was chased away by a wind that stayed firmly at high altitudes, and the sun beamed down in none too subtle invitation.

After she'd washed up she donned her oldest pair of denim shorts and sandshoes, applied insect repellent and sunscreen, pulled a hat over her head and began to explore her domain, scrambling up beside the little creek until she found the low ledge of rock that marked the tide line.

There were mangroves, which had by now dwindled in size and number, disappeared entirely, to be replaced by the source of the sweet smell that teased her nostrils each evening—thickets of wild ginger, dense and impenetrable, forming a wall across the creek and thrusting up into the bush on either side. Picking a spray of delicate cream flowers, she tucked it behind her ear and turned back along the edge of the mangrove swamp.

They were such distinctive trees, their leaves olive-yellow against the trunks and strange black breathing roots spiking up in their thousands through the spongy tan mud. Between the roots, holes of all sizes and unknown origin echoed with abrupt and frequent clacking noises.

She could see movement, and by looking from the corners of her eyes managed to discern crabs, small, wary and the exact colour of the mud. She'd never heard of crabs that made a noise.

'Mind you,' she said aloud, looking about her, 'I'd believe anything of a place like this. "Sinister" is definitely the word.'

The yellow cast to the trees, she discovered, squinting as she peered at them, came from tiny flowers that studded each one. A faint waft of scent encouraged her to walk out along an old log washed down the creek by some long-ago storm.

Carefully she leaned out as near as she could go to the mangroves. Inhaling deeply, she closed her eyes for a second, all the more to enjoy the scent, strong and sweet and distinctive. Yes, she thought, the mangroves combined with the ginger flowers to perfume her evenings gloriously.

And that was when a piece of the log broke under her foot, tossing her into the glutinous embrace of the swamp.

CHAPTER SIX

INTENSE revulsion jerked her upright, but by the time she'd flailed herself onto the comparative firmness of the bank she was covered in the sticky, smelly stuff. Her skin crawling, she made her way as fast as she could to the beach.

It seemed to take forever, and by the time she got there she was almost gagging. Walking out into the tide, she tried to rub away the stinking gunk, her face rigid with loathing. It was soon obvious that if she wanted to get anywhere near clean she had to take off her clothes.

It was simple enough to yank the T-shirt over her head. The sandshoes were a bit more difficult, but eventually she managed to wrench them free and toss them onto the sand. Thanking heaven that her shorts were old and easy to intimidate, she began to ease them down past her hips. After a few moments of struggling, she realised that she was going to have to remove her briefs as well. She hadn't worn a bra, for which she was devoutly thankful, so, naked and shivering in spite of the heat of the sun, she set to work and scrubbed the mud from her clothing before flinging each item after her shoes.

Pleased that they landed exactly where she aimed for, she told herself smugly that Anet, who'd won an Olympic gold medal, hadn't been born with all the athletic ability in the family. Dipping her head under, she rubbed her wet hair until it was as clean as the sea could make it.

In spite of the chilly bite of the water it felt good to be unhampered by clothes. Nudists, she thought as she walked towards the shore, certainly had a point. She was looking down at the tiny waves dragging against her feet when some atavistic instinct thundered a warning through every cell in her body. Her head whipped up, each hair stiffening in its follicle.

And there, standing by the corner of the bach as though he had just come around it, was Kear.

Jan's hands flew to cover herself. They were not enough, and she cringed as his heated, hungry gaze swept her body, then flicked up to her face.

Run, every instinct screamed. Get the hell out of here!

His big body was locked in the unmoving, predatory patience of a huntsman; the sun turned his hair to old-gold, outlined his strong features with a brutal impersonality. Odd snatches of images reinforced Jan's mindless, primitive fear—a boldly lustful Viking, a knight carrying a sword in a mailed hand, a laughing, bearded pirate, all unconstrained by the puny leash of morals or law, imbued with the hunger to possess.

Like an animal facing death, she stopped breathing, her skin chilling as adrenalin pumped through her. For long, charged moments they stood motionless, eye unable to leave eye, while the sea ran unheeded across her narrow feet, crisping to foam around her toes. Shivering, persuaded by some primal reflex to minimise her exposure, she sank to her knees.

It was then that she saw him cage that first, unguarded reaction and impose an iron will on his appetite. As relief and a clandestine wicked regret flooded through her Kear said in a voice that echoed unevenly in her ears, 'Stay there and I'll get you a wrap.'

He wasn't gone more than a few seconds. Without looking at her or speaking he put the towel on the dry sand above the high tide mark and strode back into the bach.

Clumsily, shivering, she huddled into the towel.

You're overreacting, she told herself, bewildered by the extravagance of her response. OK, you're not in the habit of rising like Venus from the sea, stark naked except for a few wisps of foam around your hips, but for heaven's sake you're a sophisticated woman! And Kear is not a lustful idiot, all hormones and no self-control.

It didn't work. However hard she tried to reduce those few moments to the mundane, she could still feel the potent effect his gaze had had on her, the smouldering intensity that had burnt up the air between them, draining it of oxygen so that, dry-mouthed and painfully exhausted, she felt as though she'd run a marathon.

He was waiting outside the bach, standing with his back to her. Jan stopped.

Equally swiftly, his head turned. He must have hearing as sharp as an animal's, she thought, lifting her chin to meet his flinty gaze.

'It's all right,' he said quietly, without expression. 'You're quite safe.'

'I know.' The words sounded curt but shaken. 'Next time, though, how about tooting your horn?'

'I walked down the hill. You'd better get inside and change into something warm.' His gaze moved to the heap of muddy clothes she was carrying like a shield in front of her. 'What are those?'

'I fell into the mangroves,' she said, and even managed to produce a laugh. 'Which was why I was cavorting around out there. It seemed easier to wash the mud off in the sea.'

His jaw stiffened. 'Give them to me,' he said. 'Noelle can put them through the washing machine.'

'No, washing by hand will actually do the job better.'

'Jan,' he said, his voice thickening into a low rasp, *'get into some clothes.'*

She shot inside and into the bathroom, ran water into the primitive old bath and soaped every square inch of her body, lathering her hair and rinsing it several times, finding some sort of comfort in the habitual movements. What she was doing, she realised with a shock, was scouring every trace of his hot, intent scrutiny from her skin. At last, pinkly shining and waterlogged, she dried herself and pulled on her robe.

One glance from the doorway revealed that the bach was empty. Nevertheless, she almost ran into the bedroom, where she dragged on a pair of jeans and a long-sleeved shirt with fingers that were clumsy and slow. After combing her hair she put on lipstick.

All right, she told her reflection silently, it's only a gesture at armour, but I need it.

She had every reason not to trust herself. Her eyes were a dilated, sleepy blue, and her lush mouth throbbed while the fiery lick of forbidden anticipation still prowled through her veins, singing a siren call to destruction.

Later, when she'd regained some poise, she'd deal with that inner treachery. Right now she needed attitude. Lifting her head, she gave the woman in the mirror a swift, cool, confident nod, and went out into the other room.

Kear had put the kettle on the range and was making coffee. As she came in he looked up, his eyes frozen, his expression clamped into severity. 'You'd better have this,' he said distantly, holding out the steaming mug. 'I'm sorry I startled you.'

Startled? Oh, if only that had been her sole emotion! 'It's all right, you weren't to know,' she said. With hands that trembled slightly she lifted the mug to her lips, although the liquid was far too hot to drink.

'What were you doing in the mangroves?'

'I wanted to look at the flowers. I didn't know those malignant-looking trees had such exquisite little flowers, and so beautifully scented. I followed my nose, inched out along a log and leaned over to look at them—and the wretched log dumped me into the mud.'

'I like mangroves,' he said. He waited until she sat down before seating himself, but in spite of the easy casualness of his answer his eyes were still guarded. 'Scientists have discovered that they're of vital importance to the ecology of the sea.'

Jan nodded. 'I know, I know; they get a bad press. But honestly, they don't really *try*, do they? They don't do *anything* to make themselves more attractive.'

His answering smile warmed her down to her toes. Oh, God, she thought wearily. You're getting in too deep here, you idiot! Terrified, she hurried on, 'What makes the loud cracks I hear when the tide is out?'

'Snapping shrimps,' he said. 'They live in the holes in the mud.'

She sipped some coffee, alarmed to discover that it had lost its flavour. All she could taste was danger, hot and persuasive on her tongue. She felt wired, her skin pulled tight against sinews and nerves that were taut with expectancy.

Flight or fight, she thought, but it wasn't entirely that. When Kear had looked at her something had splintered inside her, each tiny piece invading her with a cargo of hungry need that ate into her self-possession like scalding water slicing through ice.

And he'd felt it too, she thought, sickened by the depth of her gratification. Was it just desire, the urge a man felt when confronted with a woman who was nicely packaged? Or something more complex?

And was this feeling she had for him as simple, as easy as desire, or had she at last taken that first scary, electrifying step out into the daunting, untracked realms of love?

She had nothing to judge it by, nothing to compare it with. Only once before, when she was twenty and green as grass, had she thought she was in love, and she'd soon found out her mistake.

She didn't want to have to cope with this. Until she'd seen Kear at the polo ground her life had been enjoyable and gratifying. Just by existing he'd sent the whole satisfying edifice tumbling, filling her with suspect, reckless thoughts and emotions and sensations.

'I didn't realise shrimps could make noises,' she said casually.

She suspected that he knew what she was doing, because his answering smile was a nice blend of satire and understanding.

'These ones can,' he said. 'Are you going to drink that coffee or cuddle it?'

Caffeine was weak and useless compared to the effect Kear had on her, but obediently she lifted the mug to her mouth.

He said, 'I came to ask you to dinner tonight.'

'I can't, I haven't brought anything to wear!' Although she knew she was being foolish, she couldn't suppress her violent disappointment.

His brows lifted. 'Try a sack,' he said drily. 'You look superb in whatever you happen to have on, as I'm sure you know.'

She shifted in the chair, alerted by some darkness in him, a pent-up energy that prowled beneath his cool dominance.

'Thanks,' she said, 'but the sack would need a lot of work done to it. I don't think—'

'It's not formal,' he said brusquely. 'My cousin and her husband are staying the night and I thought you might like to meet them.'

She should refuse politely. Jan thought she'd opened her mouth to do so, but she said, 'Well, if you don't mind me arriving in the only dress I packed.'

His smile was pointed as a knife-blade. 'I don't mind,' he said as he got to his feet.

An undertone to the words brought Jan's gaze up to meet his; she saw nothing in the ice-grey depths but a hint of self-derision that bewildered her. 'What time?' she said, rising also because he towered over her.

'I'll pick you up at seven,' he said.

'You don't have to do that,' she objected. 'I'll drive up.'

'There's a heavy rain warning out, and the Land Rover will deal with your hill better than that toy you drive.'

Before she could protest further, he said, 'By the way, that damned ginger has just about choked your creek.'

'I know. I saw it just before I fell into the swamp.'

'Did you know it's a noxious weed?' When she shook her head, he went on, 'Yet another of the collection on this place. That means that the onus is on you as the landowner to get rid of it. I'll tell Brett to get it out next time he goes past with the digger. Expect him in a couple of days.'

'Thank you,' she said. It was the best solution, but she'd keep tabs on how long it took, and she'd pay him for it.

Before he left she had another try at convincing him that she should drive herself to the homestead, but he said merely, 'I'll pick you up.'

'What did you say people call you? Autocratic? I think I prefer bossy,' she retorted.

He looked at her with hooded eyes, said, 'Sticks and stones...' and swung up the track, long legs covering the ground fast.

Jan waited until he'd disappeared before she followed, turning when she reached the shelter of the trees to survey the scene below. No, he wouldn't have seen her until he'd walked around the corner of the bach. The buildings and the pohutukawa trees hid the water quite effectively.

But then, she'd already acquitted him of deliberately coming down. He was not a peeping Tom. Broodingly, she retraced her steps. Her stay in the country had rapidly acquired overtones she could do without. It was almost enough to send her back to Auckland.

Because any sort of liaison between them, if that was what this was pointing to, would be hopeless except on the most superficial level. And that, she thought, deliberately making things as sordid as she could, meant that if they became lovers she would be available for him whenever he came to Auckland, and no doubt there would be occasional weekends spent here. Once or twice a year they might go away on holiday together, skiing, or sailing, or overseas.

Jan wasn't shocked by the prospect; she had seen relationships like that work apparently satisfactorily for years. What did shock her was that, besides seriously considering such a situation, she'd just found out she was starting to feel quite extraordinarily possessive about Kear Lannion.

Thinking about it would make it harder to resist the opportunity when it arose. If it ever should. And resist she'd have to, because lying in ambush beneath giddy expectancy was a greater threat. If she surrendered to this hungry passion it could damage her permanently, in ways she didn't yet understand. Kear made too much impact. He was a darkly exciting man, with the ability to cause havoc and change lives. There must be women who had wept when he'd left them, women who still thought of him with a primal thrill.

Just the sort of grief she did not need.

Setting her jaw, she took her dress from the wardrobe. High-necked, long-sleeved, easy-fitting, it was non-threatening—the sort of thing that could be worn almost anywhere. A wallpaper dress, if you ignored the way the pretty violet jersey subtly altered the colour of her eyes to a mysterious, smoky blue...

That evening, when she got ready, she was sorely tempted to emphasise into exotic provocation the slight tilt of her eyes, and fill in a red, red mouth. She didn't, partly because applying cosmetics by the light of the lamp was a chancy thing, and partly because she knew she'd be issuing an open challenge.

Flaunting her femininity would send out the wrong signals. She didn't know how Kear would respond—the thought of it sent reckless little shivers the length of her spine—but she had enough sense of self-preservation to hold back. Both she and Kear had the willpower to control the white-hot flare of attraction that arced between them; they were sensible, mature people, who understood that physical passion was no sound basis for a relationship.

'I'm too level-headed to let him cause havoc in *my* life. I wonder what you'd do?' she said aloud, opening the drawer to put her cosmetic bag back. On an impulse she undid the suede bag and shook the miniature into her hand. 'You don't look the sort to toss your bonnet over the windmill, but I'll bet you got whatever you set your mind on. Anyway, I'm not into masochism. Men who don't marry until they're in their thirties usually have some good reason for it. It's not as though he wouldn't have had the chance.'

Serene with the confidence of her two hundred or so years, the painted woman smiled back at her.

'Odd,' Jan said, 'but you have a disconcerting way of changing expression.'

A flash of lights coming down the track brought her head up. She put the portrait back and opened the door as Kear brought the vehicle to a halt. He got out and came towards her, saying, 'Turn out the lamp.'

She complied. 'Should I do anything about the heavy rain warning?'

'This place has lived through more rain than I have,' he told her laconically. 'You've shut all the windows and banked the range?'

'Oh, yes.'

'Then lock the door and we'll be off.'

It began to rain as she removed the key from the lock. Not a gentle fall either. However, Kear got her to the car without any more damage than slightly damp shoes. But then, she thought, settling into the Land Rover, he's that sort of man. I'll bet he never has to look for a parking space in town.

As they went back up the track she noticed with some alarm the small torrents of water already rushing down the wheel ruts. More to reassure herself than to make small talk, she said, 'Heavy rain always looks more dramatic in the country than it does in the city.'

'Because it's more important,' he said. 'What is an inconvenience in the city can mean the difference between life and death in the country.'

Perversely she argued, 'But there are compensations for living here.'

'There are compensations in almost anything.' His tone was coolly objective. 'I enjoy going to Auckland. I like the theatre and the galleries and the sense of occasion you find there, but I wouldn't like to live in any city. Could you see yourself living here?'

Although he was merely making conversation, her heart bumped in her breast. 'No,' she said swiftly. 'I suppose I could run my business this distance from Auckland, but it would mean a lot of travelling. I'm used to a fairly frantic pace of life, but not to constantly being on the move. And I'd miss my friends and family.'

'I'm sure you would.'

Chilled by the matter-of-fact note in his words, she settled back into the seat. Without actually saying so, he'd just made it clear that there was no future for them because their lives were so different. And she'd agreed. Her heart contracted so painfully that for a moment she was fooled into thinking that it was real agony.

Rain poured down, great slanting sheets of it turned to silver by the lights. Jan tried to banish an aching melancholy by observing, 'It looks like a cloudburst.'

'Cloudbursts are few and far between, but even if it is, don't worry. We only have a couple of creeks to cross, and they're not big ones.'

However, when they got to the first one she realised that the water was much higher than earlier in the day. 'I suppose it drains away as fast as it rises,' she said, twisting around as they crossed the bridge.

'Usually.' He didn't seem worried, and sure enough, by the time they arrived at the homestead the rain had stopped, and huge, bright, newly washed stars were springing out across the dark reaches of the sky.

Kear's cousin Penny was a doctor, her husband Derek an accountant, both were in their late thirties. With a slight shock, Jan realised that Penny Andrews was pregnant.

Nobody said anything about her state, but Jan noticed that her husband was protective, as was Kear. A strange pang of loss, or longing, swept through her. Calm down, she told herself, it's just your biological clock ticking away.

Although not exactly the truth, it was easier to treat it like that. She didn't envy Penny her baby, but it stood as a symbol of commitment and happiness—things Jan had given up on.

No, she told herself robustly, you haven't given up on happiness. Don't be an idiot—a woman doesn't have to be married to be happy. You were perfectly contented until—oh, until Anet fell in love with Lucas.

And envy was too strong a word to describe how she'd felt then. She hadn't begrudged Anet a jot of her happiness; she'd just wished that she too could find someone with whom to share such a joyously passionate tenderness. Perhaps a lingering remnant of that longing had sensitised her, so that she'd been ready to notice Kear, tall and lithe and all male, the first time she saw him.

Jan enjoyed the evening. Judicious questioning revealed that Derek Andrews was a distant cousin of a friend of Jan's, so they had a little in common to smooth any awkward moments. Not that there were many of those—Jan had learned from her mother how to make people feel at home. In fact, she had to make a conscious effort not to take over the position of hostess.

It rained several times during the evening, more fierce downpours that made her look uneasily across at the windows, but the sky was clear when they said their goodnights. As Kear drove her back, Jan stared out through the window at the silent farmlands until the Land Rover came to a stop outside the bach.

'Thank you,' she said at the door.

But he came in with her just the same.

'You're not likely to find intruders,' she said, smiling, perhaps slightly light-headed at his closeness.

'I know, but it has happened,' he said absently as he lit the lamp.

The tension that had assailed Jan all evening returned tenfold. Anticipation set her nerves smouldering, shredded the composure she had thought ingrained. The lamp laid a warm, mellow patina of light over them both, finding the fire in the depths of his hair, accentuating the lines of his face, the sculptured strength of his jaw and cheekbones, the proud poise of his well-shaped head, and his mouth—ah, God, his mouth.

Hunger so intense it was like compulsion tore through her. Her eyelids felt weighted and heavy, her throat dry. Licking her lips to soothe their intolerable heat and sensitivity, she struggled for control. Her breasts rose and fell with her swift, shallow breaths.

Then he turned, and saw what she had spent so much time and effort hiding, even from herself.

In his sudden, alert stillness, in the deliberate restraint of his harsh features, in the ice-rimmed eyes, she saw the same battle, the same desperate willpower trying to leash the demons before they broke from their cage.

'Damn,' he said in a rasping, impeded voice.

'Go home.' She despised the betraying tremor in her words.

'Jan—'

'Just get out of here,' she whispered furiously, backing away.

A slight movement caught her attention; fascinated, appalled, she watched those long, lean hands clench into fists as he fought to subdue the emotions that were consuming him. And then he said, 'Goodnight,' and walked past her into the night.

It was entirely appropriate for the heavens to open at that moment. Lightning flamed garishly across the sky as a crack of thunder so loud it made her yelp drowned all other sound.

Jan pressed the back of her hand to her mouth, stifling a hysterical need to call out Kear's name. The headlights of the Land Rover stabbed through the darkness, were reduced to nothingness by another ferocious flare, another crash of thunder.

It never thunders like this in Auckland, she thought ridiculously, unable to close the door.

The vehicle didn't move. She peered anxiously through the night until a blue-white flash revealed Kear running fast and low against the rain.

'What's the matter?' she cried, falling back to let him in. He was drenched, his hair sleeked against his head in a black cap, his shirt plastered against his shoulders, trousers clinging to heavily muscled legs and his eyes glittering in his wet face.

'This could be the start of a cloudburst,' he said swiftly, bending so that she could hear him. 'We might not make it back home, but we can't stay here either. Water's starting to run across the flat. It looks as though the creek's blocked somewhere up the hill. That damned ginger, probably. We don't want to be caught in a flood. Grab your sleeping bag.'

'My—my car,' she stammered.

'We can't do anything about your car—it won't go up the hill now. Get the bloody sleeping bag,' he snarled. 'Move.'

Thoroughly unnerved, she ran into the bedroom, snatched up her sleeping bag and was ready to run back when, obeying a feverish prod from her unconscious, she pulled open the drawer and found the miniature. Clutching it, she raced across the bach; Kear blew out the lamp, yanked the door closed behind him and picked her and the sleeping bag up.

Although his arms and shoulders curved protectively around her, by the time they got to the vehicle she was wet. He pitched her into the front seat, and as she scrambled across to the other side followed her in.

More lightning lit up his face, savagely angular, intent and purposeful. Without saying a word he set the Land Rover into motion and drove steadily towards the hill. After huddling into the sleeping bag, Jan sat shivering, her eyes wide as they took in the yellow, foaming streams now surging down the track.

Rain fell in solid sheets, a vertical mass that drummed viciously onto the vehicle. It had been merely toying with them before. Now, with no wind to carry it away, it could last until the cloud had lost its entire burden.

He stopped the Land Rover just below the crest of the hill; sheltered by the bush around them, they were far enough from the creeks to make sure they wouldn't be swept away by any flood. Thunder rolled and lightning spat and hissed, exposing both land and sky with its malevolent glare. It was difficult to believe there was nothing personal in that ferocity.

Kear stripped off his shirt; reluctantly, knowing she couldn't stay in her wet clothes, Jan shed her dress, thankful that it was easy to take off. Her bra and briefs would dry reasonably quickly, but the dress wouldn't.

Muttering unheard maledictions, she wrestled with the uncooperative sleeping bag. Before she had a chance to share it with him, Kear pulled her over into his lap and tucked the soft, dampish folds around them.

After a few moments the flexible skin beneath her cheek heated enough to chase away the cold. His heartbeat settled into a rhythm echoing the rise and fall of his chest, and, although Jan wasn't foolish enough to believe they were entirely safe, she began to unwind.

And with relaxation came insistent messages from her senses—delight at the heated skin against her cheek and shoulder, pleasure in the elemental scent that was part rain but mostly Kear. The soft, tenacious goad of her own desire, a heady mixture of hunger and compulsion, sparked off forbidden needs and desires and images.

Guiltily aware that she wasn't the only one so affected by their nearness, she tried to pull away.

'Stop wriggling,' he said deeply.

She couldn't so much hear him as feel his voice reverberating through the walls of his chest.

'Sorry,' she said, and summoned all her strength of mind to pretend she was somewhere else, somewhere safe, where she couldn't be seduced into insanity.

More lightning lit up the scene—coldly, inhumanly bright—and, although the thunder pounded the vehicle as much as the rain did, Jan was entirely content as long as she was being held like this in Kear's strong arms, enfolded by the primal heat of his body.

A particularly noisy rumble of thunder made her flinch. 'Sorry,' she mumbled again.

His chest lifted; she felt the hard clench of his body, and then he tipped her face with a merciless finger and kissed her.

In those forbidden, free moments just before going to sleep, when fantasies were permitted because they would soon be forgotten, Jan had wondered what it would be like to be kissed by him.

Other men had kissed her, but this kiss was something so far out of her experience she might as well never have been kissed before.

His mouth was firm, and he didn't try to force his way into the secret sanctuary as other men had; instead, he touched her lips with small, warm, infinitely comforting kisses, and she forgot the storm roaring outside, forgot that Kear was dangerous, forgot her good resolutions, the prompting of her common sense, forgot everything but his mouth and the prowling need inside her.

Eagerly, expectantly, she kissed him back. Instantly the pressure changed, claiming rather than seeking.

Thunder blended with the sound of their heartbeats, tumultuous, shattering the fragile shell of her composure until she gave him what he wanted—no, she didn't *give*... She demanded as much as he did, responding with ardent, total surrender and victory to the heated insistence of his kiss.

Across the lace of her bra his callused fingers left a trail of excitement, setting fire to her so that she thought she must glow incandescent as the lightning.

Nothing had prepared her for this wildfire rapture; nothing had ever given her such driving, uncomplicated pleasure. When he bent his head and kissed from the length of her throat to the tender curves of her breast she shuddered, her body swept by savage, unrestrained feeling, pure and keen and as terrifying as it was rapturous.

He found her hands in the folds of the sleeping bag, and, guiding them onto his chest, commanded, 'Touch me, Jan.'

Pierced by delight, she stroked feverishly over his chest, her painfully sensitive fingertips and palms tingling at the subtle friction of hair and skin. As he drew the throbbing tip of her breast into his mouth she groaned and arched her back, her body poised on the brink of some unknown precipice.

His hand slid down to the tiny, deep indentation of her navel, and that light, almost casual caress added another dimension. He found the narrow bones of her hips, the silky skin of her thighs, caressed them with expert gentleness, and all the time his mouth exacted its toll of her body, pushing her further and further towards a culmination she had only ever dreamed of. She tensed as his questing fingers slipped beneath the lace of her briefs and approached the fiery, expectant centre of her need. Quivering, she waited.

Slowly, maddeningly, he probed, moved rhythmically. It was the most exquisite torture. She whispered words that couldn't be heard above the cacophony outside, and as his long fingers moved deep inside they sent her hurtling across the barrier, and she groaned at the spasms of intolerable ecstasy that milked her body of all feeling but that of repletion.

He held her close against him until she was adrift in the bone-deep lassitude of satiation.

Vaguely, she understood that he'd given her a gift, one she hadn't returned, but she couldn't think, and as the thunder moved sluggishly away and the rain rattled like rifle-fire against the roof of the vehicle she drifted into sleep, to wake eventually to a slightly aching body and a feeling of enormous well-being.

The moment she realised where she was she froze, but Kear's taut voice said, 'It's all right. You're perfectly safe.'

And full recollection flooded her. Oh, God, she thought. How could she have let him do that? And afterwards—how could she have slept the night through in his arms, his heat engulfing her, her body limp in the mindless surrender he'd reduced her to?

Where, when she needed it most, was her aplomb, her ability to cope? Gone. Somehow she'd have to summon a gritty pride from the depths of her soul, because acting with the *savoir faire* of a fourteen-year-old after her first kiss wasn't going to accomplish anything but further humiliation.

Warily, she tilted her head. His early-morning beard gave him a villainous air that did something potent to her insides. But when her eyes met his she shrivelled. His were remote, cold as polar seas. He didn't need to tell her that he regretted what had happened the night before; she read it as clearly as he no doubt intended her to.

Well, she regretted it too. And the only way to get through this was to play it lightly.

'We're going to have to stop waking up like this,' she said, her voice rusty and slow.

'You certainly make your sleeping partners suffer,' he said. However, his smile held no amusement, nothing but the wintry rejection that was tearing her heart to shreds.

She pulled away from the seduction of his heat and strength, shivering as she settled onto her own side. He got his shirt from the back, and as he donned it she wriggled into the damp, uncomfortable embrace of her dress, half turning away from him to peer through the condensation on the windows while her fingers stumbled over the buttons. The sodden landscape looked remarkably untouched by the night's fury, but she asked, 'What's happened?'

'It's going to be a fine day,' he said calmly. 'We'll go down and make sure the bach is all right, and then I'll head for home.'

But before they had a chance to move a heavy bulldozer came ponderously over the hill, and he said, 'Here's Brett.'

Moving swiftly, but without any appearance of undue haste, Kear got out and waited, positioning himself so that he blocked Brett's view of the interior of the Land Rover. Fumble-fingered, Jan nevertheless managed to finish buttoning her dress before sitting very still to watch the two men through lowered lashes and try to talk herself into some sort of composure.

After all, what had happened? Merely the sort of lovemaking indulged in by adolescents all over the country every Saturday night.

Except that 'merely' was entirely the wrong word to use. Nothing in her life had affected her like the maddened minutes spent in Kear's arms last night. Yet it was obvious from his attitude that it meant very little to him.

Forcing her mind away from the sense of betrayal clawing at her self-esteem, she made herself listen to their conversation.

'Any slips?' Kear was asking.

'Three,' the young man told him. 'None of them bad, and I've cleared them. The creeks have gone back down. I saw a couple of logs that need to be dealt with, but so far there's nothing serious. Max said he thought we might have a bigger slip up in the titoki paddock. He's gone off to have a look.'

'We're on our way to the bach,' Kear said. 'You'd better go ahead.'

When he'd got back into the Land Rover Jan said, 'I hope my car's all right.'

'It's not likely, I'm afraid,' he said.

Not for Kear any feel-good platitudes, she thought, somehow heartened by this. Although he might consider her to be physically fragile, he didn't appear to have any doubts about her ability to deal with a disaster.

Almost immediately they began to see signs of the storm's fury. The ruts in the road had been scoured into ragged channels, and by the time they reached the flat land behind the beach Jan was almost prepared for what she saw. Water had surged over the grass, leaving shingle, thick yellow mud and clumps of vegetation behind. Her car was still in the shed, which was on slightly higher ground than the bach, but when she climbed stiffly out of the Land Rover she could see that the water had come halfway up the wheels.

The flood had washed through the bach at a depth of four inches, leaving behind a thick wet carpet of foul-smelling mud. Jammed against one outer wall, a couple of logs were overlaid by ginger stalks, the lush leaves and fragile flowers shredded by the force of the water.

Jan said woodenly, 'I'm glad I wasn't here.'

CHAPTER SEVEN

BRETT HOPGOOD nodded. 'Woulda' been a scary night,' he offered.

Kear said, 'You can stay with me until we get this cleared up. No, don't go in there. I've got boots in the Land Rover; I'll get your clothes.'

So appalled was Jan by the devastation that she accepted his authority without any demur.

'Tough luck,' Brett said earnestly. 'It's a miracle the bach wasn't swept away. Lucky it was low tide when it happened.'

Kear appeared with an armful of clothes, which he dumped into the Land Rover. 'Come on,' he said, after one searching look at Jan.

Without protest she obeyed him. He spoke to Brett, then got in behind the wheel.

'It's not the end of the world,' he said.

She turned her head and glared at him. 'Not to you,' she said, and added, 'Well, not for me either, I suppose, but it's bad enough!'

'That's better,' he said, and dropped his hand over hers in a warm clasp. 'I'll take care of things. Don't worry.'

Normally she'd have told him that she didn't need a keeper. This time, however, she turned her cold hands to give his strong fingers a slight squeeze. 'Thank you,' she said with a wry half-smile. 'I'll be my usual self in a few minutes. Coping with my first experience of nature in the raw seems to have knocked a bit of stuffing out of me. Temporarily.'

'Floods do happen in Auckland,' he said as he started the engine.

'Yes, I know. But somehow it's not so—so immediate.'

'You'll feel better after you've had some coffee,' he promised.

Because he wanted her to she laughed before subsiding into silence, more shaken than she cared to admit. But at least Kear no longer looked at her with expressionless eyes.

Indeed, he seemed to have recovered from the chilly remoteness of those first waking moments. All the way back to the homestead he kept up a lively, amusing conversation that stopped her from dwelling on the devastation at the bach.

They were met by Noelle and the Andrewses, all concerned, all talking at once.

'We're both fine,' Kear said, reaching into the back to scoop out the load of clothes he had rescued, 'but Jan needs a shower and several cups of strong coffee, in that order. Penny, take her up to the apricot bedroom, will you, and stuff her under the shower. Noelle, go through these clothes—I think some are a bit mudsplashed.'

He didn't shout, he didn't even command, but he reduced the turmoil into order, and within a few minutes Jan found herself standing naked under the shower, shivering as reaction gripped her.

Waves of weariness broke over her; she had to force herself to wash, rubbing the soapy facecloth over her skin until she stopped shaking. Then slowly, moving with an irritating hesitance, she switched off the water and dried herself with a towel from the heated rack.

Noelle had put her clothes on the chest beside the elegant bed, underwear and outerwear sorted into two neat piles. Grimacing at the thought of Kear scooping out the contents of the wardrobe drawers at the bach, Jan pulled navy trousers and a soft navy and camel shirt over clean bra and briefs, then washed her cast-offs in the handbasin.

'Thank heaven for heated towel rails,' she said aloud.

Amazingly, the view from the window was one of autumnal peace. The glinting blue and silver waters of the harbour lapped at the beach, setting off lawns and hills of so vivid, flaunting a green that it almost hurt her eyes. It seemed totally impossible that last night's violence had happened.

And this room, charming and elegant, with its pale peach walls and apricot and yellow curtains, its antique, cast-iron curlicues at the head and foot of the bed, its fabulous linen—not too lacy and elaborate, just *right*— its antique Davenport and the subtly hued peach and blue and beige Chinese rug, almost as big as the room, didn't belong to the aftermath of a night of elemental force and power.

Holding onto her composure, Jan left the room and walked down the splendidly carved and carpeted wooden staircase. Some of Kear's art collection hung on either side, each painting carefully placed. He was clever; he had chosen works that fitted his glorious house. If he'd bought anything outrageous, he must have hung it elsewhere.

Halfway down she realised that he was waiting at the bottom, watching her with eyes that were flat and grey and unreadable.

'All right?' he asked.

She nodded, alarmed by her desire to go into the haven of his arms and stay there. It had to be all these antiques, she thought almost hysterically, her gaze slipping past his to rest on an elegant Georgian hall table and mirror; she'd regressed to times when women were frail and cosseted—and exploited, her brain reminded her acidly.

In a voice that held nothing but impersonal politeness, he told her that coffee was ready.

Pinning a smile to her lips, she braced herself to meet them all. However the sunny morning room was empty except for a table set for breakfast.

Kear seated her, then said, 'Noelle's made kedgeree, but if you don't feel like eating anything so substantial, there's yoghurt and fruit.'

'That sounds lovely,' she said.

She drank orange juice and spooned out grapes and kiwifruit and fresh mandarin segments nestled together in a pretty glass bowl. 'Where is everyone?'

'Penny and Derek are making sure their flights are in order. I shouldn't think they'll have any trouble; this was just a localised cell of rain, and from the radio reports it was barely five kilometres across.'

'Has there been much damage?'

'Surprisingly little,' he said, offering her toast. 'Surface water, a few slips on the roads, some houses flooded—but none, I think, as badly as the bach. Oh, Brett tried your car; the carpet's soaked but the motor goes. He's going to drive it back so he can put it over the pit and get a better look at the damage.'

Apparently Kear had no intention of discussing what had happened the previous night. Neither, dear God, had she.

Although she'd been quite sure she couldn't eat anything, the food had put fresh heart into her. Pouring coffee, Jan said, 'Thank Brett for me, but I'll organise its repair—the man who normally looks after it will say rude things to me if I let anyone else touch it. He's an MG fanatic.' She said belatedly, 'And I haven't thanked you. If I'd been there alone I'd have been terrified.'

'Possibly, but you'd have coped,' he said calmly.

It was the highest accolade she'd ever received, she thought, recognising just how dangerous her response was. Mesmerised, she sat with her eyes snared by his, feeling them widen and widen until his compelling, decisive face filled her vision, filled her heart and mind. She opened her mouth to say something, something utterly embarrassing and disconcerting, something that would humiliate her afresh every time she thought of it for the rest of her life.

Fortunately a sound from outside prevented it. When Penny walked in, Jan clamped her mouth shut and offered devout thanks to whatever angel happened to be looking after her.

'All well?' Kear asked, standing to pull out a chair for his cousin.

'Yes. Derek rang the Automobile Association and apparently the roads are clear. It's been raining all through Northland, but nothing like it did here. We'll stick to our original plan—drive down to Whangarei and catch the plane from there.' She looked at Jan. 'How are you feeling now?'

'Much better, thank you.' Which came perilously close to being a lie. As Kear had sat down again she'd been struck by a realisation that dazed her.

I'm in love with him.

'You'll be all right,' Penny said cheerfully. 'Kear will deal with everything.'

Kear didn't seem to think this declaration was unusual, perhaps because his natural dominance had been allied to great responsibility at an early age to produce the person he now was—a man to whom everyone looked for leadership.

Even Jan, when confronted with something she'd had no experience of, had meekly given in.

She said crisply, 'I'll go down this morning and see what I can do.'

'No,' Kear said. Unimpressed by Jan's startled glare, he went on with infuriating logic, 'I don't want anyone inside the bach until it's been checked for structural damage. I'll ring a builder before I leave the house and I'll take you down myself after I've checked out the damage around the station.'

It had been a long time since anyone had so calmly vetoed her plans. Jan said colourlessly, 'If you give me his name I'll ring the builder,' and drank some more coffee, failing entirely to get her usual satisfaction from its taste.

She might be in love with him, she might suffer an extraordinary mixture of anticipation and resentment each time he looked at her and whenever she thought of him, but he had a few things to learn about women.

Penny said, 'You're more likely to get good service if you let Kear ring. Do as he says,' she advised, not without sympathy. 'He's always right—he's made a habit of it.'

His smile was a nice blend of understanding and mockery. 'It's not a simple question of right and wrong, it's just setting priorities. Unfortunately for Jan, Papanui comes first.'

'I understand,' Jan said, trying to sound casual. 'Of course it does. I'm rather single-minded about my career too.'

His mouth compressed, but he said evenly, 'So that's settled. I'd better get going. If you want to use the phone to ring anyone in Aukland, feel free. When are you and Derek leaving, Penny?'

'Just after midday. I think Derek— Ah, here he comes.'

As the Land Rover took Kear, Derek and the ever-faithful Sheba off on a reconnaissance of the farm, Jan said, 'Well, Kear or not, I think I'll walk down to the bach and get to work.'

Penny looked alarmed. 'Do you think you should? I know Kear wants you to stay here.'

Jan considered herself far too well-balanced to indulge in defiance for defiance's sake, but this observation set her teeth on edge. 'Kear is inclined to be a little too protective. I'm sure that the sooner I get on with it the easier it will be to get rid of that mud. And I'm not a total idiot—I'll be able to see if anything's dangerous.'

Penny looked at her for a moment, then nodded decisively and said, 'I'll come with you. In fact, I'll drive you down.'

Jan thought of those ruts in the road. She looked at Penny, remembered her pregnancy. 'It might not be safe to take a car down there,' she said.

'Then I'll walk down with you.' Penny gave her a wide, genuine smile.

Jan knew when she was beaten. So she spent the morning ensconced in a pleasant little conservatory overlooking a garden where blue and white balloon flowers bobbed in the borders against echiums and lavender and late dahlias, all remarkably unaffected by the rain.

Penny was intrigued by Jan's career. She made a good job of hiding it, but Jan detected a slight overtone of amusement whenever she referred to it. Not that Jan was surprised; many people, especially those who held professional qualifications, thought it an essentially lightweight, frivolous way to earn a living. However, when Penny began to talk about it she followed suit.

After a while Penny said thoughtfully, 'I can think of several women—and not just patients in my practice—who need someone like you. Medicine is nowhere near as stuffy and hidebound as it used to be—we do take note of holistic healing now.'

'It doesn't happen all that often, but I've seen women transform their lives,' Jan said. 'With the best will in the world we seem to bring up so many of our daughters with poor self-esteem.'

'Have you a daughter?' Penny asked, apparently idly.

'No, but I have a half-sister, and because she was different from me I felt sorry for her. So I protected her, thereby convincing her there was something wrong with her.'

Penny nodded, her hand coming to rest on her stomach. 'Well, if this one is a girl I plan to give her an enormous amount of self-esteem. We Lannions are brought up to think there's nothing we can't do.' She smiled reminiscently. 'I can remember when I was eight or nine and Kear was only six; I climbed the big jacaranda over there, and he couldn't—his arms weren't long enough to reach. He wasn't going to be beaten, so he spent the entire Christmas holidays trying to get there.

In the end, with sheer determination and a bit of lateral thinking, he managed. That was typical of Kear. He doesn't give up easily.'

A small frown puckering the smooth skin between her brows, she watched her fingers pleat the hem of her shirt, then slid a swift sideways look at Jan and said with the air of one making up her mind, 'I think that was why he took the breakdown of his marriage so badly.'

It was stupid to feel as though she'd been betrayed. Ridiculous.

So, disregarding the powerless rage that surged through her, Jan said lightly, 'I hadn't heard of a marriage.'

'It's one of his few failures,' Penny sighed. 'He married an utterly enchanting English girl about five years ago. Glorious-looking, a real darling, and so in love with him. But she couldn't settle here. She was used to a very sophisticated social life, a house in the country about fifty miles from London, lots of to-ing and fro-ing—Papanui seemed like the end of the earth to her. I felt so sorry for her. And for Kear.'

'An impossible situation,' Jan said, trying hard to sound no more than mildly interested.

'It was. She was absolutely besotted by him, but in the end she left. They were divorced a year or so ago.' Penny looked slightly self-conscious. 'At least there weren't any children.'

'They're always the ones to suffer the most,' Jan agreed, recalling her desperate desire for a father. She could still remember her delight when Cynthia had married again, and at last Jan had had two parents like other children.

Penny's hand came to rest protectively once more on her stomach. 'Yes,' she said soberly. 'Kear will marry again, of course, but I think he'll choose his wife a little more sensibly this time. The experience hardened him.'

'It would harden anyone,' Jan said, aware that her voice sounded wooden but unable to do anything about it. Why was Penny telling her all this? Kear's cousin did not look the sort of woman to indulge in gossip.

Jan had lost her taste for confidences, so forestalled the possibility of hearing any more by getting to her feet.

'Do you mind if I leave you now?' she asked, knowing that she was being abrupt. 'I have a couple of calls to put through to Auckland, and I'd better get them done before Kear comes back.' She smiled. 'He told me to make them, you see.'

Penny laughed. 'And Kear is accustomed to people jumping when he says jump,' she agreed.

Instead of ringing straight through to her insurance broker and the solicitor, Jan stood for a long moment in Kear's office, staring blindly through the window at the glowing day outside, her clenched fist pressed to her chest. It was impossible for her to tease out and separate the tangled skeins of her emotions, but the chief one was outrage.

And hot on its heels came a bitter, corrosive jealousy.

If she had wanted to find out exactly what she felt for him, Penny's bombshell had been just what was needed.

Damn it, he should have *told* her...

And even as she realised how completely out of line that involuntary reaction was, she wondered whether he'd kept silent because he was still bitter, still felt something for the enchanting Englishwoman who had been unable to live happily here.

God, she thought explosively, if this is love, I don't want a bar of it.

Perhaps it was just a physical need verging on the perilous border of obsession. If so, according to everything she'd read and what she'd seen of friends' experiences, eventually it would burn out. All she had to do was hang in there with a death grip on her self-respect.

But she had a horrible feeling it was more than extreme attraction, because she couldn't bear the thought of Kear being unhappy. Even if his misery was caused by another woman.

Dragging in a shaken breath, she picked up the telephone, went through the procedure to get the call put on her account and tapped in an Auckland number. When eventually she got to the solicitor he clicked his tongue in consternation. 'What a business. Where are you?'

'With a neighbour,' she said.

'That's all right, then. How are you going to get the house cleaned?'

'I can do that,' she said briskly. 'It's very small—it won't take long.'

He said cautiously, 'You must do whatever you think best, of course.'

After that she contacted the insurance firm who dealt with her car. The woman who spoke to her was brisk and no-nonsense. A local garage would tow her car out and assess the damage, if any. They would contact her.

Although it was unlikely that any Fijian newspaper would print news of a localised cloudburst in New Zealand, Jan decided she'd better contact her parents just in case. She flicked open the tiny address book she always carried in her bag, found the number scribbled on a piece of paper inside the front cover, and rang through.

Apparently her mother was lying beside the pool. Visualising her, Jan smiled a little wistfully. She'd be sleek with expensive sunscreen, under the biggest sun umbrella the resort could find, sipping a cold, non-alcoholic drink—and there would be a man somewhere. Cynthia was fiercely loyal to her husband, but men flocked around her and she'd long perfected the ability to deal with them so lightly that it prevented any jealousy from Stephen.

'Darling, what rotten luck!' she said when Jan told her about the flood. 'Are you sure you're all right?'

'I'm fine.' Jan spent a few minutes reassuring her, forbade her on any terms to come home, made her laugh, promised to take care, and hung up with a smile.

Through the window she could see Penny in the garden, stooping to clip off heads of flowers too bloated by moisture to stand upright. She carried a trug to dump the rejects in, and with her tall, graceful slenderness and the wide-brimmed hat shading her features she looked just as the chatelaine of such a place should be.

Had Kear's English wife been like that? Everything that Jan was not?

And that, Jan told herself firmly, is enough of that. Inferiority does not suit you.

She went out to join Penny, wondering irritably how long it would take the garage to send someone out to check her car. It irked her to be restricted, unable to do what she wanted, and she suspected that Kear had told his cousin to keep Jan away from the bach. Had he also asked Penny to tell her about his brief marriage?

In a way it was a relief when the Andrewses left after an early lunch; Jan said her farewells at the house, tactfully not going out with them so that Kear could say goodbye with some privacy.

A restless compulsion flicked through her, tightening her skin and irritating her nerves. She was standing in the elegant little parlour, with its beautifully panelled walls and exquisite antique furniture, when Kear came in so silently that if it hadn't been for the radar she seemed to have developed she wouldn't have known he was there.

After one shrewd, considering glance he asked, 'What's the matter?'

'Nothing.' It sounded so curt and rude she tried to modify it. 'The sooner I get the bach into shape the better.' Although her heart quailed at the prospect. She had seen enough television newscasts of weary women and men clearing up after a flood to understand what it entailed.

'We'll go down now,' he said casually.

Made infinitely more edgy by his tall, self-contained presence, she avoided his eyes and said, 'That would be great, but you don't need to—'

'Jan,' he said, a warning note in his voice, 'don't be silly.'

Nevertheless, she tried again. 'I'm sure you've got lots to do—ditches to unblock and stuff like that.'

'There's been very little damage. I keep my creeks clear, and the bush in the gullies lessens the effects of a heavy downpour. Your creek overflowed because logs caught in the ginger jammed it so that the water couldn't get away. It found the easiest path down to the sea, and unfortunately for you that happened to be through the bach.'

'I see,' she said, glad that it hadn't happened while her grandfather had been alive. The possibility of further floods did concern her, because that would certainly compromise her plans for the area.

He said curtly, 'I won't try to seduce you, if that's what's worrying you.'

Some unarticulated hope died when she looked up into his forbidding face and noted the straight, hard mouth, the unyielding features. 'No,' she said, 'I'm not worried about that.'

'Good. It should never have happened and I'm sorry that it did. It certainly won't happen again.'

Well, he couldn't have put it more plainly. There was no room for hope. As she sat beside him in the Land Rover and chatted easily about the weather she thought that of course he believed in the old adage of cruelty being kinder in the long run.

Her road had been graded into some semblance of evenness, presumably by Brett. In the moist heat the dankness and moisture had combined to produce a smell of decay.

But that wasn't the worst of it. Brett had also pushed away the logs and ginger from the side of the bach, and it was obvious that something was badly wrong. The corner drooped.

Shock drained the colour from Jan's skin. 'What happened?'

'The force of the flood skewed the building off its piles. The septic tank and plumbing aren't usable, and the tank stand is hanging on by a prayer. Jan, you can't stay here. The place will have to be demolished.'

'Poor little house,' she said, forgetting her dismay at her first sight of it. 'At least it didn't happen to my grandfather.' She turned away, too slowly to hide the tears drowning her eyes.

'Don't cry,' he said roughly.

She couldn't prevent the great sob that tore its way up from her throat, and with a soft curse he took her into his arms.

It was pure, shameful weakness, but she let him hold her while she wept for all the things that might have been and now would never be—for her grandfather and her father, for her doomed love, even for the hours of work she'd put into cleaning the bach. Eventually her brain drifted into lethargy, a golden haze where the only thing that meant anything at all was Kear's warm, strong support.

She would remember this on the day she died, she thought. The faint, potent scent that was special to him, the feel of his body against hers, lithe and rock-solid, the heat of the sun beating against her hair and the backs of her bare legs, the soft sound of the waves on the beach almost drowned by the highly acrimonious discussion being conducted by birds somewhere in the mangroves.

Seductively easy though it was to let him take over, she had to pull herself together before she forgot that apart from this fierce song in the blood they had nothing in common. He had already been burned by an unsuitable wife, and she wasn't going to risk heartbreak.

Drawing away, she said steadily, 'Thanks for that. I don't usually bawl—it just seems such a waste. I'd better get everything out of the bach that I can.'

'Everything small enough to move easily has gone,' he said. 'Noelle came down this morning and got them and took them up to the homestead.'

'I could have done it,' she said angrily.

'I know.' His smile was filled with irony, his eyes cool and implacable. 'But there was no need.'

Oh, he'd definitely asked Penny to stop her coming down in the morning, and Penny, a Lannion through and through, had been quite ruthless about it, using her pregnancy to make sure.

'Now,' he said brusquely, 'we'd better get what's left.'

There wasn't much: the table and chair, the rocking chair. Together they loaded them onto the back of the Land Rover, watched with intelligent curiosity by Sheba.

'I'll send a couple of the boys to get the wardrobe and the bed,' Kear said when they'd finished.

The sun shone benignly down, and although the white puffy clouds moved rapidly there was little wind at ground level. In fact it became so steamy that Jan was glad she'd worn shorts.

Resolutely she refused to look at Kear, because after a few minutes sweat stuck his shirt to his back and shoulders, outlining the smooth, tensile swell of muscles, the bunched strength when he had to use them. People on film sets whose job it was to make heroes look sexy could take lessons from Kear; he had a natural, unforced sensuality, immensely more potent than that of any star.

Kear said, 'Come on, let's go. You look exhausted.'

'Sad, I think,' she said. 'It's like the end of an era. I keep wishing I'd known my grandfather.'

'It was his decision.' He held the door open. 'In you get. Don't regret the past, Jan, you can't change it. Put your efforts into the future.'

It made practical, if somewhat harsh common sense. Did he take his own advice? Had the English wife who couldn't be happy here been written off like a bad investment, a cautionary tale?

Somehow the thought of him doing this hurt as much as the possibility that he might still long for her.

Halfway up the track Jan looked sideways. Outlined against the foliage of the kanuka trees, his features combined in a bold statement of raw power. The straight nose, arrogant above sculpted, disturbing lips, the strikingly defined jaw, the high forehead, all somehow added to and emphasised his uncompromising personal authority.

He wasn't handsome, she thought, trying to be objective. Her sister Anet was married to the most stunning-looking man she had ever seen—Lucas Tremaine had the sort of face that stopped women in their tracks, overawing them with his sheer physical beauty—yet, like Kear, 'handsome' didn't describe him. The word was too weak, indicating only appearance, and to most women looks weren't particularly important.

The special quality Kear shared with Lucas was a powerful charisma, the virile masculine presence that signalled to women's hidden, hereditary instincts, proclaiming that this man was strong enough to protect and tender enough to be gentle, intelligent and confident and trustworthy, and therefore a prospective mate and father.

In the unsparing, coolly critical regard of elemental femininity, Kear and Lucas were equals. Both had the forceful, disciplined authority that came from inner resources. Her stepfather had it too, as did Drake Arundell, who was married to Jan's closest friend Olivia.

Who, she recalled, had given Anet the miniature which Anet had handed on to Jan as a birthday present only a few weeks before.

Automatically she turned around.

'What are you looking for?' he asked. 'I checked the bach. We haven't left anything behind.'

'I left the miniature in the Land Rover last night and I forgot to take it in this morning.' She managed to hold her tone steady, as though it were perfectly normal for her to forget something so valuable.

'I'm sorry, I forgot to tell you. I found it this morning. It had slipped down between the seat and the back. Relax,' he said, stretching out his hand to enfold hers.

Embarrassing colour burnt through her skin. His hand was long-fingered and strong, and at that moment every place he had touched the night before glowed as though she'd been stroked with fire.

I don't know whether this is love or not, she thought despairingly, but I do know that although he wants me he doesn't feel anything like this, or he wouldn't be touching me so casually. Need gripped her, so intense it overrode all the social constraints imposed to stop people from making fools of themselves, utterly disorganising the tidy efficiency of her thoughts.

Fortunately he removed his hand before she burst into flames.

She said fervently, 'I'd never forgive myself if I lost her. Whoever she was, she should have stayed in nice, tame England, where she'd have been cherished and cared for, instead of giving in to a surprising spirit of adventure and shipping halfway round the world.' She drew in a breath. 'Kear, where's the nearest motel?'

'You can stay at the homestead,' he said evenly.

She said, 'No, I've been enough of a nuisance.'

The corner of his mouth tucked into what might have been a smile if it hadn't been so forbidding. 'I know, but why inflict yourself on some poor motelier who hasn't become accustomed to your capacity for disasters?'

She laughed, but persisted. 'I can't just dump myself on you.'

'I'd rather you stayed at the homestead. You'll be much more comfortable.'

It would be so easy to give in, but every day spent in his company would mean at least a month's suffering when she left. Probably more, she thought, wrestling with a hollow foreboding.

Primly, she said, 'Kear, I know no one bothers much about reputations in this day and age, but I really don't want to be seen as a—a—well, as your—'

He waited, damn him, until the words trailed into an embarrassing silence before saying in a flat, unemotional voice, 'Don't be silly. No one is going to assume you're a scarlet woman.'

'Nevertheless, I think it would be better if I stayed at a motel,' she said firmly, shaken by the power of her desire to give in.

Although she hadn't expected him to press the matter, she was piqued when he said indifferently, 'If that's what you really want, but the offer is still open.'

Back at the homestead he organised the storage of the furniture, then gave her the miniature. 'Do you want me to store it in the safe?' he asked casually.

She shook her head. 'No, I'll take much better care of her from now on.'

Tina, working late on some papers that had to be faxed through to Germany that night, answered the telephone and said, 'Telephone, Kear. It's from Wellington.'

Leaving them, Jan ran up to the apricot bedroom to put the portrait with her clothes, and met the house-keeper outside the door. 'Oh, Noelle, thank you very much for collecting all the stuff from the bach this morning.'

'That's all right,' Noelle said cheerfully. 'Not a problem.'

Jan liked her, but it was difficult to tell what she was thinking; part of being a good housekeeper, presumably.

Noelle said, 'Jimmy Turner from the garage rang. He said to tell you he's collecting the car in an hour or so.'

'Good. I'll have to see if I can hire one.'

Although Noelle's brows lifted, she remained discreetly silent. Probably wondering why I don't just sit back and let Kear take over, Jan thought as she went into the bedroom and put the portrait on the dressing table.

Outside, the harbour was transformed by the descending sun into a sheet of rosy mother-of-pearl. Jan stood in the window and forced herself to appreciate something that normally would have enraptured her.

Close proximity to Kear Lannion was scrambling her brain, she thought, despising her weakness. Self-preservation insisted that the faster she leave Papanui the better. It was going to be bad enough spending the next few weeks in the same district as Kear, but if she didn't get out of this glorious house with its fabulous gardens soon, she could well become so besotted with the man that she'd lose all desire to leave.

And standing here getting maudlin over him isn't going to help, she told herself. A cold shower is what you need.

She didn't go that far, but she certainly felt better after she'd showered the mud off and changed into a respectable pair of trousers and a silk shirt, combed her hair and put on a touch of lipstick.

By now Kear should have finished his phone call from Wellington, so she had no excuse not to go down and start ringing motels. Jutting her jaw, she summoned her resolution and went down the wide staircase.

Tina was closing the office door behind her as Jan came up. 'Is Kear in there?' she asked.

'No.'

Jan said, 'In that case I'll go in and make some calls. Are you on your way home?'

'Yes.' Tina smiled at her. 'It's all done, thank heavens. Goodnight, Jan.'

So it was Jan now, not Miss Carruthers. 'Perhaps I'll see you tomorrow,' Jan said, smiling at her.

Unfortunately, none of the motels nearby had vacancies. Oh, some could put her up for a night here and there, but, as one told her, 'This is a holiday area, Ms Carruthers, and we're usually booked out several weeks ahead even at this time of the year. With Easter right in the middle—well, I'm sorry, I can't help you.'

There were no hotels with accommodation closer than Kerikeri in one direction and Kaitaia in the other, neither of which could really be considered in the district.

'I don't believe it,' she said, putting the receiver down with a short crash.

'What don't you believe?' asked Kear from the doorway.

Jan had to control a nervous start before she looked over her shoulder. He must have showered too, because he'd changed from his working clothes into a well-cut shirt that made the most of his broad shoulders, and trousers that showed only too clearly the strong muscles in his legs.

Every inch of Jan, especially her fingertips, remembered the texture of his skin. Swallowing to ease a suddenly dry throat, she said, 'I can't find a single motel that has a room.'

He didn't look surprised. 'Of course, Easter is almost here.'

She nodded. An awkward silence stretched between them—awkward for her anyway. Kear didn't seem troubled by it. He was encased in the armour of aloofness that he'd donned some time in the thunder and lightning of the previous night.

'So I'm grateful for your offer of hospitality,' she said at last, stumbling a little over the words.

'Even though you'd rather not be here.' His voice was cool. 'Is it because of what happened last night?'

Gritting her teeth she said, 'Well, yes, I suppose that's part of it. But I don't want to be a nuisance.'

'You're not.'

To her ears it sounded like a meaningless formula, the automatic response of a courteous man—a conviction which was reinforced when he went on with off-putting correctness, 'Obviously I find you very attractive, but I don't make a habit of leaping on unwilling women.'

The bite in his words made her feel foolish. 'I'm not in the least worried about that,' she returned formally. 'I know you're not a rapist.'

'Your reluctance to stay here did make me wonder whether you thought you might have to fight for your virtue.'

'No!'

Not him! Fight herself, yes, and the urgent hunger he roused in her perverse and altogether too co-operative body. Chagrined because his deliberate and unwavering mastery of his emotions was the surest guarantee of her safety, she allowed herself to toy with the idea of smashing through the barricades of his self-possession. The panicky exhilaration and anticipation that flooded her appalled her into banishing the fantasy instantly.

'Then, as that's settled, let's have a drink before dinner,' he said, a cool irony underlying his words.

CHAPTER EIGHT

JAN accompanied him into the smaller of the two drawing rooms, less formally furnished than the other, with mostly modern sofas and chairs. On the walls were more of his collection. If she ran out of small talk, she thought, she could discuss those. Some she liked, some were stark and far from comfortable to look at, but all possessed a dynamic power she recognised instantly.

'Sit down,' he said. 'What would you like?'

'Soda water and lemon, thank you.' Teased by suspicion, she told herself firmly that Kear couldn't have manipulated this whole situation; masterful, even dominating though he was, the weather was beyond his control. So was the condition of her inheritance that made it necessary for her to stay for a month.

He poured her a drink and himself a beer, then sat down in the chair that was clearly his. 'Well,' he said, smiling at her with those deceptively transparent eyes fixed onto her face, 'here's to peaceful cohabitation.'

'I—yes, of course,' she said, shocked at the prim note in her voice. Lord, a single look from him and all her sophistication seeped down the drain. Leaning back in the chair, she tried to relax muscles that seemed to have locked, and cast around for something to say.

For possibly the first time since she'd been an adolescent, not a single thought came. How did he manage to turn her brain to curds?

Kear rescued her with a query about her book. Ridiculously grateful, she seized the subject, and after that things went along smoothly. But when eventually she sat down at the dining table she thought with prickly embarrassment that never again was she going to take her social skills for granted.

145

Fortunately for her composure, the rest of the evening passed just as serenely. After an excellent dinner Kear excused himself to do some office work, and Jan stacked the dishwasher then picked up the newspaper.

An hour later, just as she was finishing the cryptic crossword, he came back. 'There's a documentary I want to watch,' he said. 'Do you mind?'

'No, not in the least.'

He looked at the scrap of paper she'd scribbled the crossword answers on. 'Do it in the paper next time,' he said, sliding a door open in a cabinet at the other end of the room to reveal a television set. 'I don't have time for them.'

When the documentary—a look at world trade patterns—was over, they talked about it with the ease of old friends.

Experience had taught Jan that most men didn't like a woman pointing out the flaws of logic in their statements. They tended to get angry and defensive, and either attack or become paternal and patronising. Kear didn't. He used his formidable intellect to refute some of her arguments, but he remained good-humoured. And when she made a point he acknowledged it, and discussed it.

Later in her bathroom as she cleaned her teeth, she decided that she shouldn't have expected any other reaction. Kear's self-esteem gave him such inner security that he didn't need to be reassured of his correctness all the time.

Tempered though it was by his surprising understanding and compassion, there was a moral toughness about him that would probably make him hell to live with.

Exciting hell.

But not, she said, ignoring the signals her body was sending, for you.

Restlessness gripped her, jagging through her cells, stretching her nerves to a leaping tension.

That night she dreamed of him, and every night afterwards, and each night the dreams became more explicit and demanding, so that she woke with her body taut and the blood pumping hotly through her veins while frustration ate into her.

Yet she was oddly lethargic, letting herself drift through the days, cocooned in the golden haze of her love. As long as they didn't acknowledge this attraction, she thought, she'd survive. Oh, not without fall-out, she didn't believe in trying to fool herself. There'd be pain in direct proportion to the consuming sweetness of the time they spent together, but at least she'd retain her self-respect.

Thank heaven he kept his word and made no move towards her. One brush of those long hands on her receptive skin and she'd fly apart, and if they made love she would never be the same again. It was ironic that the ecstasy her body craved would lead inevitably, mercilessly to the anguish she dreaded.

Because although Kear liked her and enjoyed talking to her—and wanted her—she could see that nothing so world-shaking was happening to him.

He wasn't easy to read, but neither was her sister's husband, and yet when Lucas looked at Anet the intent, tender possessiveness that irradiated his turquoise eyes was unmistakable. Jan had seen a variation of it in Drake Arundell when he watched Olivia—an ardour that was both fierce and gentle, an outward expression of love from a very private man.

No hint of such emotion appeared in Kear's face. He couldn't have been a better host, but the wall was still there—the impregnable fortification of his self-sufficiency.

If she made it obvious that she wanted to go to bed with him he would quite possibly take her. He'd be a brilliant, skilful, experienced lover, who would seduce her to paradise.

Then, when the time came for her to go, he'd wave her goodbye with the inbuilt courtesy she had come to expect from him and that would be an end to it.

For him . . .

So she guarded her heart. It would be dangerous to let him realise that she shivered with inward delight when he came into a room, and utterly humiliating if he ever found out that he'd invaded her dreams. She did not want to be lumped in his mind with Gerry and Louise and all the other women who'd fallen for that altogether too potent, unruffled charm and thrilled to the concentrated strength that backed it up.

On her fifth night at Papanui Jan slid into bed, pulling the sheet and duvet up to her chin. Situated as it was between the harbour and the ocean, the homestead was never without the sound of the sea echoing in even the most enclosed rooms, and the faint scent of salt drifting on the air.

When was this lingering summer going to end? The calendar proclaimed that it was halfway through autumn, but the weather denied it with summer temperatures and summer humidity. Jan flipped over onto her side, pushing the duvet down to the end of the bed. A mosquito whined past.

'Oh, no,' she grumbled, pulling the sheet over her head.

Of course it didn't go away so, muttering, she flung the sheet back and leaned over to switch on the bedside lamp.

Ten frustrated minutes of searching later, she decided to go for the heavy artillery. She dragged her robe on and found the spray can in the bathroom. If she lived here, she thought as she sprayed the room with the bare minimum of insecticide, she'd see that the bedroom windows had screens. But of course she'd never live here.

Shafted by anguish, she set the can on the dresser and went noiselessly out through the door. In ten minutes the insecticide would have settled, the mosquito would be dead and she could come back. In the meantime she'd have a drink of water and from the morning room window watch the moon over the harbour.

The house was quiet, and in spite of the panelled walls she could see quite well. She looked along the hall to where Kear slept, but no light shone beneath his door. He was no office farmer. Although Papanui had a manager Kear did more than his share of the work outside, as well as spending hours dealing with the never-ending paperwork.

Once in the kitchen she poured herself a glass of water and walked with it into the morning room.

As in the rest of the house, the curtains hadn't been pulled. Jan stood still, the glass cool in her hand, and looked out to where the climbing moon silvered the high, bush-covered headland and the rich farmlands.

There was something about moonlight, she thought, trying to play down the languorous tide of longing, of desire and need and awe, that gathered in every cell of her body, sweeping sane, sensible logic into oblivion. The moon's tranquil beauty transformed the daytime world of colour and solidity and dimension into a for-bidden mystery, an aloof, enigmatic other world, where shadows could hide unknowable secrets.

Kear said from behind her, 'What are you doing?'

Jan hadn't heard him come in, but her body had known, had sensed his presence. So much for the magic and miracle of moonlight.

'I think I've been waiting,' she said without moving, each word huskily hesitant.

'And is your waiting over?' he asked. Level, neutral, the deep voice could have been exchanging social pleasantries had it not been for the raw edge to the words.

Although Jan's eyes still lingered on the nocturne of silver and grey and black outside, she knew he was as affected by her as she was by him. The minute he'd come through the door she'd recognised him at some fathomless, intuitive level, and had known what she was going to do. Known, and accepted its inevitability. Carefully, still watching the moon, she put the glass down on the window sill.

A slow, sweet thickening of her blood told her that this was right, this was her time. She could grasp it now and go with it, or turn her back and for the rest of her life not know what fear had driven her to reject.

Caution and common sense had done their best, but she no longer wanted to follow their drab dictates. She understood exactly what she was doing, and she would follow her hidden longings joyously, without regret, without quibbling.

'Yes,' she said simply, wishing she could say something so wildly romantic that he'd always remember this moment, never be able to expunge it from his heart and his mind.

Her desire for this man was a consuming urgency that frightened and awed her, a kindling of passion that wasn't diminished because he felt nothing so heartstopping.

Not that she blamed him; you couldn't make others feel as you did, and love that was forced was not worthy of the name. No, she'd take this for what it was— passion, white-hot and elementally charged. She'd surrender to it, and when it was over she'd remember him with kindness and regard and honour. How she hoped that he'd think of her the same way.

It wouldn't make her pain any easier to bear, but it would mean she didn't go to the end of her life shamefacedly rueing her lack of courage.

'Are you sure?' he asked, unable to subdue or perhaps not caring about the rasping note to the words that gave them such dark weight.

'Very sure,' she said, still looking out over the black and silver shadows.

He laughed, a low, deep sound that scraped deliciously along her nerves to explode in a chain reaction through her, sparking a conflagration so intense that she thought her response must glow around her like a force-field.

Fingers cupped the nape of her neck. The thumb that came to rest on the hollow beneath her ear moved slightly, and to her astonishment a runnel of fire worked its way through her. 'You have the most seductive back view of anyone I know,' he said quietly, all traces of triumphant laughter banished. 'Such a vulnerable neck, and then you turn, and one glance from those tilted flirt's eyes sends my blood pressure up through the top of my head.'

Jan's breath blocked her throat. Dimly, she recognised the noise in her ears as the hammering of her pulse, heavy and erratic. Her lips curved into a volitionless unseen smile.

Shivering at the heated touch of his mouth on the responsive skin beneath her hairline, she tensed when he trailed kisses to the sensitive point where her neck met her shoulder, those knowledgeable hands turning her slowly, relentlessly into his arms.

His seeking mouth traced the outline of her face, from high cheekbones to pointed chin, the slanted line of her eyes and brows, the vulnerable temples. He was wickedly tender, yet it was not the patronising gentleness of the strong for the weak. No, he was deliberately delaying the moment when he kissed her mouth; she knew it, and knew why. He was curbing the appetites he intended to indulge because he was a man for whom control was vital.

And she, comparatively innocent of the fiery, relentless warfare between the sexes, knew she couldn't allow this. If he took her like that, never straying outside the bounds he had set about his emotions, she'd be cheated in some basic, inexplicable way.

Until then she had stayed quiescent in his grasp, making no attempt to touch him. Now she looped her hands around his neck, pulling herself into the lean power of his body. As if her movement was a signal, his arms contracted suddenly and he crushed her mouth beneath his.

Her heart rejoiced at this sign, the first chink, but almost immediately he disciplined his hunger. The savage pressure easing, he said against her lips, 'I'm sorry.'

'Why?' she sighed, astounded at her stark, uncompromising reaction to that untamed moment.

Without answering, he kissed her once more, being very careful not to hurt her, yet the restrained pressure of his mouth shattered some secret barrier buried in her mind, in her body. He gave her no choice, he simply took what he wanted, and because this need that ravaged her was not one-sided, in her surrender she discovered a fierce exultation unlike anything she had ever experienced before.

His heart picked up speed, driving in a rhythm both primitive and overwhelming. His taste saturated her senses, his primal male scent filled her nostrils, although even as she recognised this it altered subtly, warning of atavistic changes in his body. He was readying himself for her and her heart leapt, her body springing into life, ardent with the need to take and give, to join with him in the ultimate capitulation, the ultimate victory.

Locking her like a precious burden in his arms, he picked her up and moved without noise through the silent house. With half-closed eyes Jan scanned the clamped features of desire in his face, the dark slash of his brows above glittering eyes, the hard, predatory line that was his mouth.

When he pushed open the door to his room Jan was revisited by that feeling of rightness, a rich certainty that gave her the confidence to sit up after he put her down onto the enormous four-poster bed. The grey ice of his eyes had fragmented into shards, rendering them hypnotic, unreadable and irresistible.

He bent and kissed her again, and she went under, opening her mouth to the demanding authority of his.

Dazedly, she remembered she had something to tell him. She should explain—and then inescapable fingers tilted her head back and he kissed the long line of her throat, stopping in the hollow at the base, where her life force pooled. She would wear that kiss for the rest of her life— a brand that marked her as his. Unhurriedly, with a delicacy surprising in a man so big, his free hand slipped to cup the soft, small mound of her breast.

Shivering, Jan nuzzled blindly at his neck, her whole being utterly absorbed in the excitement his clever, prac- tised hands roused. But soon her need to touch him became an urgent compulsion, goading her to push aside his shirt so that she could run her hands across the hot, sleek skin beneath.

He stiffened, his breath catching. 'Yes,' he said almost soundlessly. 'I've spent long, lonely nights remembering just how it felt when you touched me—how you quivered beneath my hand.'

'Yes.' Jan turned her face to kiss the muscle that flexed against her cheek. On a shaky indrawn breath she mur- mured, 'I'd know your scent anywhere.'

'Yours haunts me. Sweet and piquant, with an under- note that promises all the seductions of Delilah, so faint it should be impossible to recognise, and yet I notice it even when you're no longer in the room.' He removed her dressing gown swiftly.

Then he looked at her, his eyes burning like pale, bril- liant crystals behind the dark frame of his lashes. So disturbingly intent they were, the remoteness somehow magnified by a devouring heat, that Jan shivered once more.

'You're cold.' He tugged the sheet over her, and shrugging off his clothes came into the bed.

Jan had dreamed of this moment, fantasised about it both awake and asleep, and she truly thought she had no more resistance. But, however vivid, dreams and im- agination were unable to vanquish the painful memories of the first time—the only time she had made love. When she went rigid Kear gathered her in his arms, and for long, humming moments lay with her, giving her time to get accustomed to the virile strength of his body.

I will not be hostage to this damned fear, she thought, and forced herself to relax, to batten down the memory, banish it to the most distant regions of her mind. This is Kear, she repeated, like a kind of mantra, over and over again.

And this was her decision.

It took an action of his to drive the fear from her. He cupped her breast again, the long fingers curving to lift it before he bent to suckle the waiting bud. Sensation lanced through her, absolute, acute, sharp enough to be next door to pain, converging between her legs and building until she was wound so tightly she thought she would explode.

Delicately, in spite of his work-hardened hands, he explored her body once more, making his the curve of her hips, the indentation of her waist, reacquainting himself with the satiny skin on the inside of her thighs. Jan's head spun, the turmoil destroying coherent thought as that merciless mouth at her breast, the tender, implacable hand on her body, urged her closer and closer to some unknown, secret mystery.

She couldn't bear it, she thought, clutching at him.

'Please,' she said, in a voice high with strain.

His hand drifted down to gauge her readiness. 'Yes,' he said harshly, lifting his head.

Jan had never felt like this before, never wanted anything so much that she could have killed for it. The moment he delayed to put on protection was a frustrating aeon. Even that buried fear stayed quiescent; her dazed eyes adored the way the moon slid across his skin in a sheen that made him more than human, only slightly less than a god. She ran a questing forefinger up the muscled flank, and smiled hungrily at the way his skin flexed beneath hers.

It wasn't until he turned that panic flickered into the forefront of her bemused brain, and by then it was too late.

'It's all right,' he said, seeing, as usual, more than she wanted as he eased himself over her. Unerringly, he read the reason for her sudden sharp breath, her involuntary flinch. 'Trust me, Jan. I won't hurt you.'

Years ago someone else had said that to her, and he had been wrong. But with cold memory darkening her eyes Kear touched her again, preparing the way, and as she tensed at his gentle expertise he claimed her, and with slow, careful increments pressed into her.

It was like being taken over, an exacting, inexorable invasion. The sensuous indolence he'd engendered fled to be replaced by terror, unreasoning and blatant. Jan heaved upwards, her hands pushing at the powerful shoulders, her face desperate.

'What is it?' he said, his voice stark with barely leashed passion.

She couldn't speak, couldn't do anything but thrash her head from side to side, trying frantically to dislodge him.

Beads of sweat stood out on his brow. 'Jan,' he groaned, and she realised to her horror that she had gained what she'd thought she wanted—the breaching of his wall of restraint. Retreating inside herself, she scuttled away into the furthest recesses of her brain. The flicker of understanding in his eyes was overtaken by a ruthless need as he thrust deeper, stretching her delicate tissues unbearably.

Her gasp echoed through them both.

'Are you all right?' he asked roughly.

The feeling of intrusion, of being dominated, taken and used, was fading. Although it still felt strange, he wasn't hurting her. The feverish hunger he had roused was replaced by relief.

'Yes,' she whispered, saying the word with such astonishment that it could have been the first time she'd ever used it.

It seemed that he had regained control, for he began to withdraw. Paradoxically, when she understood what he was doing she clutched him and muttered, 'No.'

'It's all right,' he said, an odd, unreadable note in the words. 'I should have thought—you're so small. I must frighten the life out of you.'

'No,' she repeated, more positively this time, but he turned over onto his back, using his great strength to carry her with him.

'Do what you want,' he commanded, his voice deep and husky and sure. 'Take what you can.'

Bewildered, alert and wary as an animal tempted by something it didn't understand, she moved experimentally. And suddenly it rushed back, the eagerness, the singing in her blood, the raw response, untamed, inciting. Sensation shuddered within her, grew into a sweeping lazy fire that pulled at her breasts and made taut her languorous muscles.

She said hoarsely, 'Touch me, Kear.'

His hands moulded her breasts, a thumb across each flowering areola. Jan's hips rotated, and once more anticipation roared through every nerve-end.

'Yes, you like control,' he said relentlessly, his hands closing on her breasts, then sliding down to bite into her narrow waist. 'Take it, Jan, enjoy it, and ride it for all it's worth...'

Once more she began to move, to enclose him, and this time there was no threat of old, remembered agony, nothing but an exquisite need that conquered her, reducing her to incoherence and a blind, mindless craving while strands of tension began to twist and tighten inside her, summoning her higher and ever higher. She saw nothing but the clenched lines of Kear's face, ferocious with the compulsion that drove them both together to some unattainable goal.

Only it wasn't unattainable; her body convulsed with delight, with wonder and rapture and an enormous, selfish sense of being given more than she could endure, an unbearable ecstasy that rocketed her over the border into boundless, inconceivable pleasure.

It couldn't last; slowly the waves of sensation began to fold back onto themselves, but still she moved, fascinated by the unsubtle angularity of his features, the hard dominance that making love didn't soften. He was all male, his skin dark against hers, his hands at first gentle on her hips and then, when the need got to him, the strong fingers clenching almost to cruelty.

She saw the moment he forgot he'd ceded control to her. Sweat gleamed across his shoulders, across his brow. Beneath the dense lashes his gaze locked with hers, molten silver duelling with blue. A harsh sound was torn from his throat and the great bow of his body arched, muscles and tendons flexing in sinuous might.

Jan gloried in her power, wrapped in the complex joy he had given her. He cried out her name, and the last of her defences shattered into splinters inside her.

Eventually his eyes opened in smoky indolence; he looked at her astonished, delighted face and laughed. There was humour in it, but beneath the humour she thought she detected a savage note, and her joy and happiness ebbed. Confidence seeped away as she began to realise some of the consequences of what she had just done.

Something of her feelings must have shown, because he tucked her against his shoulder and asked, 'What is it?'

'Nothing. Just—thank you.'

His lips were warm on her forehead. 'Were you a virgin?'

She didn't want to answer that, yet perhaps she owed him the truth. 'Not—exactly.'

He didn't say anything. After a moment spent dreamily listening to the slowing thud of his heart, she went on,

'When I first made love I—well, we—found out I had
a very strong hymen.'

'I see,' he said. His arms tightened around her. 'It
hurt.'

She shivered, remembering just how awful it had been.
'I fainted,' she admitted. 'I had to have it cut by my
doctor.'

'And so you wonder each time you take a new lover
whether history is going to repeat itself?'

So humiliating had been the experience, and she had
endured so much pain, that in spite of her doctor's attempts at reassurance she had never gained enough confidence to make love again. Perhaps when she knew Kear
a little better she'd tell him that...

Savage sorrow gripped her. They had undergone the
most intimate, the most personal of all encounters. Yet
she was too wise to expect more than this transient
physical pleasure. She loved him, but Kear was a very
private person, who hid huge parts of himself behind
that sophisticated, self-assured exterior. Beyond
passion—and, she hoped, liking—she had no idea what
he felt for her.

'It's silly,' she said, hoping she didn't sound evasive.

'Far from it. I imagine that the first time you make
love is just as important for a woman as it is for a man,'
he said. 'Heavy with a kind of symbolic magic.'

He might not have intended it, but his next movement
was impregnated with just such symbolism. He ran his
hand from her forehead to her mouth, traced the soft,
slightly swollen outline of her lips, swept the length of
her throat, across the feminine contours of her breasts
and waist and down her hip and thigh—a gesture of utter
possession.

His voice was deep and sure and compelling. 'It's a
wonder you weren't terrified. I wish you'd told me.'

Reaching around to touch his back, Jan pressed her
palm against the warm, fine-grained skin over muscles
bulked by constant use. He could break her in two, and

yet he had been tender and perceptive, and in spite of the disparity in their sizes they had fitted together like a hand and its glove.

'It's rather hard,' she said, dry humour warming the words, 'to bring into the conversation.'

'I suppose it is,' he said slowly. 'I'll never hurt you, Jan.'

And he made love to her again, with unhurried, intensely controlled sensuality that suddenly, at her reckless instigation, spilled over the edge into uncontrolled passion, wildfire, primitive in its intensity, a fierce exchange of desire.

She woke the next morning to find herself naked in her own bed, her nightgown and wrap draped over a chair.

Disorientated, wits lost in a sensuous cloud, she stretched, and knew immediately where she had been and what she had done the night before. Colour scorched her skin, but the smile she saw in the mirror when she went into the bathroom could only have been called smug. And her eyes were drowsy and satisfied, slumbrous with a purring repletion.

Sometimes, she thought, her eyes fixed onto the shadowy marks around her waist and on the female curve of her hips, he'd only just managed to control his passion. Her smile turned to lazy reminiscence. A few bruises were payment enough for last night's ecstasy. Besides, she hadn't been entirely blameless.

Flushing at some of the more intimate memories, she turned on the shower. She did not recognise herself in the woman who had behaved so wildly, heedless of anything but the slaking of her desire, yet although she should be wondering where this sudden affair was headed, she didn't regret a single moment of the night before. She couldn't see beyond the man who had introduced her to such earthy, demanding sensuality.

Kear wasn't there when she went down to breakfast, and the house was empty of his presence. Jan was starving, so, hiding her disappointment, she ate a fruit salad made of the scented flesh of feijoas and amber-and-wine tamarillos, and small, brilliant segments of mandarins splashed with white yoghurt, tangy and delicious. Then she demolished a slice of toast and drank two cups of coffee.

Everything, she thought wonderingly, tasted so much better than it had yesterday. And surely she had never seen a sky of such radiant colour before, or a garden where the last of the roses lifted sweet, resplendent cups to pellucid sunlight, where the lawn positively radiated the quintessence of all greenness?

The fantail that flitted through the twigs of the tree outside the window was more than an ordinary bird; its pied plumage had something mythical about it as it twittered and chirped and flicked its fan-shaped tail. A messenger from unknown gods, perhaps, welcoming her to a new world. And it was entirely appropriate that two superb rosellas flew like arrows across the lawn, their brilliant scarlet and blue and yellow plumage prismatic in the sunlight.

If this was what sexual fulfilment did for you, no wonder people became addicted to it!

After breakfast she made her bed and tidied her room, then went down to the office. For a few minutes she surveyed the silent computer with a dreamy smile, then gave up the attempt to do any work and went outside, walking into the heart of the glowing morning in a haze of joy.

She found a seat carefully placed to take advantage of a view of the sea framed by massive branches of pohutukawas, and sat there for long moments, letting delight soak into her soul.

Quite when she heard Kear's voice she didn't know. He appeared to be dictating something, and she thought with a special thrill of fellow-feeling that he hadn't been able to stay inside either. She leaned her head back, letting the sun play on her face, until she remembered guiltily that even in autumn the sun was dangerous. Especially for people with skin like hers.

Languidly she got to her feet and followed his voice through a bank of oleanders, some still carrying the last of their silken poisonous flowers.

Just when she realised what he was saying she didn't ever recall; she knew only that by the time she understood it was too late to back away—too late for anything but the suspicion that stole over her on its vile cat-feet.

'Yes, she'll sell.' Not dictation; he was talking to someone on his mobile phone, of course. The person on the other end said something and he laughed. 'No, they haven't had a chance to contact her. She's been staying in the house with every call monitored, and I've been with her whenever she's set foot outside the property. A very satisfactory solution all round.'

He listened, and then laughed again. 'Penny, even I can't organise floods. But of course I took advantage of it. I don't want damned developers on my front doorstep.'

Motionless, Jan shook her head, trying to drive out the sound of his voice, trying to convince herself that those overheard words didn't mean what she thought they had.

'Why should she want to keep it?' he was asking. 'She has no ties to the place except very tenuous sentimental ones. And I'll offer her a fair price—above government valuation.'

Pain cut through Jan's heart. Stopping a cry with the back of her hand, she stood huddled for a moment, then turned and without noise walked away through the sweet-smelling garden, beneath trees planted by Kear's forebears, past flowers and skilfully planned borders, and all the while her head throbbed with her attempts to deny what she'd heard.

Surely he hadn't deliberately seduced her so that she'd sell him her grandfather's land?

She cringed at the remembrance of his lazily amused voice, the utter confidence in his tone.

No—he couldn't be so cold-blooded. But what did she know of him, really? That he was a fiery, inventive, experienced lover, who knew when to use tenderness, when to be masterful; that he was a dominant, determined man with far more than his share of masculine attraction.

That he was ruthless.

Such a man might well have decided that the simplest way of ensuring that developers didn't sully his corner of paradise was to sleep with the land's new owner and dazzle her into signing it over to him. Shame and anger seared through her; if she hadn't had her own plans for the land she might well have been so overpowered by the dark enchantment of his lovemaking that she'd have sold it to him.

She walked through the lush garden until she found herself beside another seat, this one high on a cliff overlooking the entrance to the harbour. Collapsing into it, she gazed sightlessly out to sea, shivering while she tried to work out what she should do.

After a while she looked down at the watch on her narrow wrist. Moving stiffly, she got to her feet. The thought of the coming confrontation made her feel sick, but she had to face it.

He met her coming across the lawn. After one swift, burning glance he demanded, 'What's the matter?'

'Nothing,' she said automatically, unable to prevent her mouth from curving into a bitter smile.

'Regrets,' he guessed.

She shrugged. They were standing like enemies, a few paces apart, eyes duelling. 'Oh, yes,' she said, fighting back the spilling, turbulent words. Recriminations would only make her look even more foolish than she'd been. This was business for him, so she would make it business for her too. 'But regrets are for the stupid.'

She saw the tic of a muscle in his jaw, the guarded watchfulness in his eyes.

'Did I hurt you, Jan? I'm sorry if—'

'No,' she said wearily.

He gave her a narrow smile. 'No bruises?'

'None that I didn't ask for,' she retorted with spare self-derision.

His gaze rested for a heart-shattering moment on her mouth, still slightly swollen and tender. 'I'm sorry. It wasn't entirely one-way, though. I found bruises and scratches and—'

'I don't want to talk about it,' she interrupted, cold with newly engendered shame. Last night the vehemence of their lovemaking had thrilled and excited her. He hadn't hurt her then—it had taken a few overheard words to wound her heart to the death.

His face softened. 'Jan, how many lovers have you had?'

'That's none of your business.'

'I think perhaps it might be. If I embarrassed you last night I'm sorry.'

'You didn't,' she said, trying to sound worldly and casual. The humiliation cringing through her was caused by her own behaviour.

'You make me do things I'd never have believed I could,' Kear said starkly.

Recalling some of those things, Jan felt colour surge into her face. The primitive passion that had overtaken them the night before could not be love; love needed time to flower and fruit, it needed nurturing and care, the gentle watering of consideration and thoughtfulness.

They had been willing victims of an elemental hunger that burned everything in its path, as glorious and savagely ferocious as a bushfire. And, because it wasn't based on trust, like a bushfire it left behind a blackened, smouldering wasteland of the spirit.

She said quietly, 'I overheard you talking to Derek. When did you learn developers might want to buy my grandfather's land?'

Watching him closely, she noted the flicker of comprehension in the pale eyes, the subtle withdrawal into remoteness. He didn't move, but stood surveying her with a hard, unsmiling look. 'The day of the flood,' he said.

'How much were you prepared to offer me for it, Kear?'

With no hesitation he told her. It was more than fair; it was an extremely good price for a hundred acres of reverting coastal land with no buildings.

Jan subdued the irrational rage that possessed her, fuelled by a grief so strong she could hardly contain it. 'All your precautions were wasted,' she said in the exhausted tone of ultimate anguish. 'I have no intention of selling it—not to you, not to a developer. I have plans for it.'

'What plans?' he asked curtly.

'I'm going to establish a camp there for girls who need to improve their self-esteem.'

'By which you mean girls in trouble with the law,' he stated inflexibly.

'Some of them,' she admitted. 'Not all.'

'You're unlikely to get planning permission.'

'Is that a threat?' she flashed.

'That's not how the system works. However, almost certainly you'll have the whole district against you, and the council is legally obliged to take their views into consideration. It will be a long, hard row, with little likelihood of a favourable decision at the end of it.' He spoke deliberately, his hooded eyes fixed on her face in a gaze that intimidated her by its very lack of emotion.

'Nevertheless, I'll get there,' she said stubbornly, knowing he could read the high colour in her cheeks, the bleak disillusion in her eyes.

'Have you thought how much it will cost to set up a place like that?' He spoke reasonably, a businessman pointing out the flaws in someone's project. 'You're talking millions—unless you're going to put them all under tents, which is not a good idea for a place like Northland where heavy rain can fall every season. Even then you'll need cooking facilities and ablution blocks. None of them come cheap.'

'I'll manage.' Thankfully, even to her critical ears her voice sounded calm and confident. That mindless rage was ebbing now, leaving her almost shaking with an adrenalin overdose. Swallowing eased her dry mouth, but she couldn't do anything about the ache behind her eyes.

She had never seen him like this before, good looks overshadowed completely by bleak determination, the angles of his face hard-hewn and implacable.

Making love to him was quite possibly the most stupid thing she'd ever done in her life. She despised him, but oh, she wanted him.

Yet, even then, when he was shattering the fragile, barely conceived edifice of a happiness she had never expected, she couldn't wish it undone. For ten years, traumatised by the pain of her first encounter with passion, she had held back. Because love involved physical surrender, she had refused to allow herself to love. Fear had limited her life, reduced her options, made a coward of her without her realising it. It seemed bitterly ironic that the man who had freed her had also broken her heart.

'How will you finance such an undertaking?' Kear asked.

She said abruptly, 'I'll sell the miniature.'

'You will not,' he said, the words a harsh threat.

Welcoming the first crack in his armour of detachment, she shrugged. 'I happen to think that the camp is more important than any sentiment,' she returned caustically.

'Come with me,' he commanded.

CHAPTER NINE

At her stubborn refusal to move he grasped her elbow, stated curtly, 'There's something you should see,' and swept her inexorably into the house and up the stairs. Outside her bedroom he said, 'Get the portrait.'

Without speaking, her back rigid with resentment, Jan went in and picked up the little painting from the dressing table.

Silently they continued on past his bedroom to another room, smaller than his and Jan's, but decorated by an expert with love and great taste. 'Take a look at that,' he said, pointing to a picture on the wall.

Jan came to a stop before the framed watercolour. Her incredulous eyes refused at first to accept what they saw; after a moment she glanced down at the portrait in her hand. Yes, the one on the wall was a copy—done, she saw, by a gifted amateur. Her wondering gaze took in the signature—N. Lannion, 1919—before flying to his face.

'What is this all about?' she demanded.

'That,' he said evenly, 'is a copy of a miniature that has been in our family since it was painted in the eighteenth century. It was stolen almost forty years ago, and since then we haven't heard anything about it.'

'I certainly didn't steal it,' she said furiously.

'I'm well aware of that. Nevertheless, it *was* stolen and it belongs to me.'

Normally Jan would have given it to him without a thought, but if she handed it back she might just as well sell him her grandfather's land, because she'd probably never be able to find the money to set up a proper camp unless she begged it from her stepfather. And it had become important that she do this thing on her own.

Besides, the arrogance of his final statement set her teeth on edge. Generations of privilege rang through his tone.

Swiftly, before she had time to think things through, she said, 'It's not going to be quite so easy, I'm afraid.'

'What the hell do you mean by that?' His leashed dark fury bombarded her, battering at her composure.

Anxiously, her fingers tightened around the portrait. 'I want to know what the legal position is.'

In a level, almost bored voice he said, 'The legal position is this: I can prove that the miniature belonged to my family. I can prove that this is the miniature that was stolen. Legally and morally it belongs to me. You won't be able to sell it because I've alerted everyone who might be interested, and they won't buy it from you.'

Colour drained from her skin, leaving her cold and sick beneath the outrage. He had made love to her knowing this; the experience they'd shared had been tainted by his knowledge and her ignorance. Although she'd known that for him it had been no more than passion, a carnal need, she'd thought it an honest hunger. How wrong she'd been.

If he'd felt anything for her beyond a cheap and opportunistic desire, he'd have told her about the miniature and he wouldn't have gone to so much trouble to hide the prospect of the land development.

'And,' she said silkily, 'I suppose somewhere in that desk of yours, just waiting for my signature, is a legal document giving you the right to first refusal of the land?'

His mouth hardened. 'Yes.'

No doubt he'd thought that a woman in the throes of physical passion would be much easier to manipulate. Presumably he'd planned to broach the subject when he'd thought her too overwhelmed by his sexual expertise to be able to think straight.

And if she hadn't had her own plans for the land she might well have signed it.

Oh, you fool, she thought acridly. You stupid fool!

Jan knew how it felt to have your trust destroyed. It hurt every cell in your body. It corroded the anger that came so swiftly, revealing it for the fake it was—an emotion she'd whipped up to hide the pain of betrayal.

'I'll match any offer you get,' he said. 'This is too far away from Auckland to make a good site for a camp. It's also far too big. Once you've sold this you'll have enough money to buy land not too far from Auckland. If you buy it inland you won't have to pay the inordinate amount a beach frontage commands, and you'll be able to use the extra money to put up buildings and buy a vehicle to take the campers to the beach.'

She stared at him with a peculiar blankness. His calmly logical words were somehow the biggest betrayal of all, making a hideous mockery of the time they'd spent talking, the quiet, infinitely satisfactory exploration of each other's minds and attitudes. She had allowed him to get closer than any other man, revealed thoughts she'd hidden almost all her life, yet he didn't understand her at all.

Each word as distinct and sharp as a sliver of glass, she said, 'You've got it all worked out, haven't you? I'm still not convinced that you have a legal claim to the miniature.'

'She belongs here,' he said, and there was such confidence in his tone that Jan almost winced.

'Prove it.'

He said, 'Tucked in between that wooden frame and the original frame should be a slip of paper with a few lines of verse written on it in tiny, crabbed handwriting, so faded it's very hard to read.'

He quoted:

> *'I found Love as you'll find yours,*
> *and trust it will be true,*
> *This Portrait is a fated charm*
> *To speed your Love to you.*

> *But if you be not Fortune's Fool*
> *Once your Heart's Desire is nigh,*

*Pass on my likeness as Cupid's Tool
Or your Love will fade and die.'*

Jan stared at him, then down at the miniature. A shadow of irritation seemed to pass over the sweetly wilful face. Setting her teeth, Jan undid the clip at the back of the frame and slid the miniature free. Sure enough, a piece of paper fell into her hand. She unfolded it delicately and looked down at the words. Faded, crossed, they danced in front of her eyes. She couldn't read them, but she didn't need to. Wordlessly she held the miniature out to him, renouncing all claim.

He took it, but his other hand grasped her wrist. 'Jan, listen to me—' he said harshly.

He was going to make excuses. She couldn't bear to listen. Interrupting, she asked, 'Who was she?'

He hesitated, scanning her face with a flat, intent gaze before saying reluctantly, 'Her name was Maria Lannion. She was the only child of a rich baronet, a man with a very good opinion of himself. She fell in love with her second cousin, Nick Lannion.

'His father had married beneath him and been turned off by his family, so he had no money and practically no social standing. His mother was the daughter of an artist, possibly an artist herself, and she must have passed on the talent to him. Nick earned a reasonable living as a miniaturist, but even though he was fashionably popular he was not a suitable match for Maria.

'However, she wanted him and he wanted her, and after a considerable amount of intrigue and heavy-handed parental intervention she ran away with him. They were married in the traditional manner over the anvil at Gretna Green, and although her father cut her off without a penny their marriage was extremely happy. Their great-grandson was my great-grandfather.'

It was Maria Lannion who'd handed those straight black brows on to her descendents, as well as the firm jaw and the imperious air of determination that went with it.

Not hiding the bite in her tone, Jan said, 'I want a receipt.'

'Certainly,' he said frigidly. 'Come down to the office and I'll give you one.'

Good, she thought judiciously as they descended the stairs in silence and went into the office. She didn't care about his anger. He had a damned nerve to expect her to trust him.

When he handed her a sheet of paper she didn't even bother to read the words. 'Can you tell me how I can hire a car from here?' she asked, folding the receipt with meticulous care before putting it in her pocket.

'Why the hell do you want to hire a car?'

'I'm going to have to buy a tent.'

She thought she heard him swear, then he said roughly, 'Hang on.'

Jan watched as he dialled a number. 'Gavin?' he said curtly. 'It's Kear Lannion here. Do you have a unit you can make ready for someone? Right, I'll bring her down.'

She said slowly, 'I should have guessed, I suppose. I didn't realise just how much power you had in the district.'

He didn't look embarrassed. Grey eyes remote as winter, he said, 'It wasn't difficult—most of them were booked out over Easter, and the others knew they'd have enough casual travellers to fill their rooms.'

'Why didn't you tell me when you first saw it that the portrait was yours?'

After a moment's pause he said indifferently, 'I wanted to find out the legal position.' Then his expression changed, and with it his tone. 'Jan—'

'Very sensible of you. I'm ready to go,' she interrupted, because the last thing she wanted was a post-mortem, and if he tried to justify himself she'd probably burst into tears and humiliate herself utterly.

Although someone had arrived at the homestead expecting to be shown some stock, Kear insisted on driving her to the motel. He didn't speak much, and then only what had to be said, but when she'd signed in and he'd taken her suitcase into the unit, he said, 'We have to talk. I'll come down tonight.'

'I have nothing to say to you—' she began.

'I have plenty to say to you.' Although his face was guarded and grimly invulnerable, his tone revealed something of his determination. 'I'll be down at six. We'll go out to dinner somewhere.'

But she had left long before then, heading down to Auckland on the bus, determined to give herself some breathing space.

'Running away,' she admitted aloud, safe in the sanctuary of her home. Possibly. Oh, all right, definitely. But she needed time to form some sort of skin over her wounds.

The telephone was ringing when she unlocked the door. The answering machine was on, so she ignored it. Sure enough, it was Kear, his voice arrogant and cold. 'Ring me when you get in,' he said, and hung up.

He rang three more times during the evening, disturbing her scratch meal, her shower and a vicious bout of tears. She didn't answer.

Eventually she went to bed, to lie for hours staring at the ceiling, listening to the noises of the city, aching with grief. Strange that Olivia and Anet had both found their loves after acquiring the portrait...

Some time during the night the telephone woke her. She struggled up through layers of sleep, dimly aware of a headache and such extreme lethargy that for long, frightening moments she didn't know where she was. Damn, she thought hazily, scrabbling for the telephone, she should have left the thing on the answering machine.

It had to be Kear; he wasn't accustomed to being denied. Picking up the receiver, she croaked, 'Please stop harassing me.'

His anger scorched down the telephone lines, edging every word. 'What's the matter? Your voice—'

'I'm just *tired*. Leave me alone.'

And that, she thought as she replaced the receiver, was the last she'd hear of Kear Lannion. She had spent thirty years of her life without knowing he existed; she hoped fervently that it would be as long before she saw him again.

Three empty, solitary days later she travelled north by bus and collected her car, once more in mint condition. Jan should have been pleased, but she had lost the capacity to feel. She couldn't allow herself the luxury of expressed emotions, so she kept them safely walled away.

Before she'd left Auckland she had called on Mr Gates, the solicitor, who, scandalised by the flood, had agreed that staying at a motel three miles away would fulfil her grandfather's condition. He also told her, far too late, that he'd been approached by a consortium interested in buying the land.

'You can't, of course, do anything about it until you have possession, but you should think about it,' he said.

Jan promised to.

The first morning in the motel she didn't do anything more than go through her notes, only to discover that she couldn't bear to work on them. So after a meagre lunch she got into the MG and drove along to her land.

She saw no one. To her mild surprise the bach had been cleaned, all the mud and slush and filth washed out completely. It was a relief, because she hadn't wanted to go there and find the ruin that had driven her to Kear's home. However, it also meant that she was even more beholden to him.

The weather had finally decided that it was getting close to winter. Instead of sunny, mellow days and warm rain, cloudy skies cloaked the hills with sombre veils of showers. Wind, crisp and chilling, ruffled the harbour into grey waves. Beside the bay the mangroves crouched, sinister and sullen.

Shivering, she got into the car and drove back to the motel.

*   *   *

Determination kept her slogging away at her notes, even when she was sure she was being utterly presumptuous by thinking they might be publishable. She didn't go out except to the motel shop to buy food. Kear didn't ring or come near her.

At last the month was over. Thankfully, every nerve in her body strung taut, Jan retreated to Auckland, vowing never to set foot north of the Bay of Islands again. After intensive thought she'd decided that Kear, damn him, was right. She'd sell the land and buy a smaller, cheaper block closer to Auckland. All she had to do now was decide who to sell it to. Kear, or the consortium. Revenge whispered seductively to her, but she suspected that in the end she'd sell it to Kear.

Her parents returned from Fiji. She went back to work and filled every spare moment with writing. Winter blasted in, bringing rain and stinging southerly winds and more rain. In a single delivery she received four postcards from Anet, all posted in different places. She appeared to be enjoying Venezuela enormously.

Jan learned that she could get by on a few hours' sleep each night, even when pain gnawed at her heart, and also that concealer didn't hide anything from her mother.

And a hundred acres of Northland farmland, busily reverting to coastal scrub, became legally hers.

As well as writing, and discussing the book with an agent who seemed convinced she could sell it, Jan undertook a hectic programme of seminars and workshops and talks, until Olivia Arundell, who had been given the miniature before handing it on to Anet, invited her to lunch three weeks after she'd got back.

After some minutes of watching Jan push delicious food around her plate, she said gently, 'Fine-drawn is all very well, but you're starting to look as though you're sliding down the slope to thinness. Cynthia is worried sick about you, and so am I. What's the matter?'

'A man, of course,' Jan said, trying to sound flippant.

Olivia looked at her keenly. 'Who?'

'The owner of the miniature,' Jan said, and explained. Oh, not everything, but because her friend was intelligent as well as kindhearted Jan knew she'd read between the lines.

'Good heavens, what a story,' Olivia said when she'd finished. 'I think Drake's father bought it in an antique shop. I suppose the curse—if that's what it is—doesn't affect Maria Lannion's family.'

'The possibility of being cursed certainly didn't seem to worry Kear,' Jan agreed wryly.

'And you're in love with him. Why isn't he in love with you? Men keep falling in love with you all the time. What's the matter with this one?'

Jan gave her a slow, ironic smile. 'He was far more interested in the hundred acres my grandfather left me. And the miniature, of course, once he'd seen it. Maria might have done her best for us, but she's getting old now, and I think she must have used up all her magic on you and Anet.'

Olivia homed in on the one thing Jan hadn't told her. 'Why did you run away? That's not like you.'

'He betrayed me,' Jan said icily.

There was silence until Olivia sighed and said, 'People think you're placid because you don't rave and shout and throw tantrums, but of course they're wrong. You have a quick temper and fast reactions—you've just learned to control them. Does he know that you're in love with him?'

'God, no,' Jan said, shuddering. People said that talking over your pain and anguish helped. It wasn't that way for Jan; just saying the words twisted something inside her. 'I overheard him discussing the land with his cousin. Kear knew that some development group was interested in buying it, but he made certain they didn't get to me.'

Olivia looked intrigued. 'You mean he kept you a prisoner?'

'That's a bit too dramatic, but yes—although I didn't know it—to all intents and purposes that's what I was.'

'Did you ask him for an explanation?'

Jan lifted a hand, then dropped it. 'I didn't have to. He admitted what he'd done without any sign of shame or remorse. As well, he didn't say a word about his claim on the miniature until he'd put the word around so that I couldn't sell it. He told me that, Olivia. So I left. I could understand about the land—no farmer would want a development on his doorstep, with right of way across his property. But the miniature—he should have told me,' she finished wretchedly.

And he had no right to make love to me so sweetly.

'It seems,' Olivia said quietly, 'absolutely outrageous behaviour.'

'There was no room for misunderstanding, believe me,' Jan said, unable to hide the bitterness in her voice.

Her friend lifted her head and frowned. 'And he hasn't contacted you at all? Not even to buy the property?'

'Oh, yes. As soon as the place was legally mine his solicitor contacted mine with an offer.'

'What about the developers?'

'They want to buy the place from me for about twenty thousand more than Kear offered, but it's conditional on planning permission being given. They want to cut it up into sections.'

'What are you going to do?'

To her complete astonishment Jan burst into tears. Olivia hugged her and let her weep, patting her back until Jan hiccupped into silence and pulled away. She said, 'I don't want ticky-tacky houses spoiling the bay. In a reluctant sort of way I felt I belonged there.'

'And that's always been a problem for you, hasn't it? Belonging.'

Jan looked at her with lifted brows and a slight frown. Before she could answer, however, Olivia went on, 'Has it ever occurred to you that every man in your life except your stepfather has abandoned you? And that much as Stephen loves you and you love him, he can never be your real father?'

'Liv, have you been reading one of those self-help, cure-the-reader-of-every-major-neurosis-in-ten-short-minutes books?'

Olivia disclaimed any such choice of reading material, and they went on to speak of other things before Jan allowed herself to be persuaded to stay for dinner.

It was a pleasant evening. Jan found herself laughing with the children, and joining Olivia and Drake in their congratulations for Philips, the man who was their greatest friend and who cooked, cleaned house and acted as nursemaid to the family. Seduced by a forthright, determined woman who had come as a gardener, he'd been shanghaied into marriage and after an extremely happy six months had just found out he was to be a father.

Back at home, Jan walked out onto the terrace. It was cold and crisp and clear, a perfect winter's night, but the stars were smudged and blurry, their pristine silver smeared by Auckland's competition.

In spite of his betrayal, she missed Kear with such intensity that she could feel it physically—a weight that came from within, a gnawing agony that seemed to increase with time. He had made love to her with a fire and passion that still disturbed her dreams, but what had he *felt* for her? It was probably just as well that she'd never know.

Reluctantly, she admitted that Olivia had hit a nerve with that last observation.

All her life she'd struggled with the fear of being unwanted, the knowledge that she really didn't belong. Perhaps that first primal abandonment when her father was killed, followed so swiftly by her grandfather's departure, had convinced her subconscious that all the men in her life would eventually leave her.

It hadn't helped that the first time she'd made love had been such a painful experience. Two virgins together, and poor Ben had been just as unsure as she was—so appalled by her pain and her eventual collapse into unconsciousness that he'd never asked her out again.

She stooped and picked a blade of lavender. Insight was all very well, but it wasn't going to solve anything for her.

Shivering, she realised that the night had begun to seep into her bones, chilling her body as Kear's Judas kisses had chilled her heart. Tucking the lavender into her pocket, she went inside, closing the door behind her. As though the gesture had reinforced some unspoken decision made out beneath the stars, she decided that the next day she'd get her solicitor to write to Kear and offer him the land.

Then, perhaps, she could give up this doomed love and get on with the rest of her life.

She woke the next morning heavy-eyed and flushed, half-excited, half-appalled by the dream that had swamped her with its heady, seductive spell. Kear, she thought, lifting limbs that were weighted with lassitude and satiation, oh, Kear!

And, wondering whether she was stupidly opening herself to more heartache, she rang the solicitor.

It turned out to be a long day, culminating in a session at the centre with the social worker and a thin, intense thirteen-year-old so desperate for inclusion in a group that she'd shoplifted to buy their attention with gifts.

It was dark when Jan left, and she was exhausted, wishing again that there was the money to do more for Michelle and all the others like her. Still, in this case she thought the girl had a good chance. Her mother was a sensible woman, and together they had mapped out a plan to give the girl some self-respect and confidence. Jan didn't kid herself that it would be easy. It rarely was.

And you, Jan told herself as she drove home, should take some notice of your own advice. Pining over Kear isn't going to achieve anything but erotic dreams and misery. Get on with your life.

Wearily, she drove into the quiet cul-de-sac, an incipient headache building behind her gritty eyes.

She barely noticed the car parked against the kerb outside her house, a dark, corporate thing that looked forbidding and powerful.

As she turned across the footpath the driver got out and waited, tall, commanding, effortlessly dominating the night.

Kear.

So astonished to see him that she almost forgot to press the button that lifted her garage door, Jan winced at the surge of heat to her veins, a swift, untamed delight that was, she scolded herself, purely physical.

He didn't come in behind her. She had to go out onto the street and say, 'Kear?'

'Ask me in,' he said, not giving an inch.

She made a little gesture towards her house and said quickly, before she had a chance to change her mind, 'Come in.'

He accompanied her through the solid door in the wall, through the small front garden with its camellia bushes and primulas, its lavender hedge and early, sweet-scented jonquils bending back from the wind. Once inside he waited until she sat before he did so. Tense, her headache swamped by an overpowering joy, she asked carefully, 'Did the solicitor ring you?'

'No,' he said. 'I came to surrender. If it takes a camp for wayward girls to get you back to Papanui, I want it there as soon as possible. You can keep the land and I'll give you the money to set it up. We'll have to fight to get planning permission, but we should be able to swing it.'

She blinked, and without even considering the offer said, 'I couldn't do that!'

'Why not?'

'Because it wouldn't be fair.'

Unevenly he said, 'I wasn't fair to you, was I? Jan, I'm sorry. I let pride and anger and sheer terror stand in my way. Can you ever forgive me?' The words were wrenched from his soul, harsh and thick and urgent, and for the first time ever she could see beneath the

shimmering surface of his eyes to the dark
intensity beneath.

She smiled through the sudden, hot tears of relief. 'Of
course I can,' she said, and walked into his arms—arms
that closed around her with such ferocity that she gasped.

He kissed her with a starved, driving need that banished all fears from her mind. He said blindly, 'It's been
total and utter hell—'

'I know.' She lifted on tiptoe and kissed the point of
his chin.

'Do you forgive me?'

'What for?' she asked dreamily.

'For being so bloody arrogant. For not telling you
what was going on. For losing my temper so completely
when you made me realise how badly I'd behaved. For
thinking I could somehow tie you to me by making love
to you—for hoping that it would be enough to persuade
you to forgive me when I told you how I'd plotted behind
your back. For not telling you that I loved you before
I took you to bed. For being a total and utter fool.'

Even to her own ears her laughter was slow and
wickedly provocative. 'I think I'd forgive you for almost
anything,' she said, adding, 'Anyway, I was the one who
ran away. I'm sorry too. I wanted everything to be
perfect—I wanted you to love me without anything else
getting in the way. But life's not like that, is it? I love
you, Kear. Nothing else matters.'

He made a low sound in his throat, a kind of feral
growl that sent shock waves blasting through her. She
looked up into eyes that splintered into heat and fire.

'Jan,' he said, and picked her up and headed for the
bedroom, finding his way by instinct.

She didn't try to stop him; that unbidden sound had
smashed through the civilised barriers she'd tried to keep
intact, the defences that were an admission of her lack
of confidence. Once in the bedroom they stripped; she
heard material tear but ignored it, goaded by an imperative as old as history, as urgent as survival.

He didn't waste time with foreplay; as though he had spent the last weeks racked by hunger, he dropped her onto the bed and thrust into her, branding her with the heat of his body, the striving urgency of his passion.

It was over too soon.

Beginning the slow, lazy slide down from the heights, she said weakly, 'Barbarian.'

'Yes,' he said quietly. 'Did I hurt you?'

She stretched languidly, feeling the sunset glow of passion like colour in her veins. 'No,' she said, yawning, and bit his shoulder hard enough to mark the sleek skin.

He laughed. 'When are you going to marry me?'

She was still. After a moment she said, 'Tell me about your first marriage.'

He turned onto his back, scooping her with him so that she was sprawled across him. 'It was,' he said steadily, 'a monumental mistake. Celia only lived with me for six months before she left. She wanted me to sell Papanui, or keep it for whichever of our children might like to live so far from London, and go back to England with her. When she left I knew that her social life was more important than I was. And my decision to stay meant that Papanui was more important to me than she was.'

Jan, accustomed to thinking of them as tragic, doomed lovers, stared at him. The fact that she loved him wasn't going to change him; he would always be hard.

And she knew it made no difference. She would go with him wherever he wanted her to go.

'You,' he said evenly, 'are different. If you want to live in Auckland I'll buy a place on the outskirts and we can work out some sort of compromise.'

Tears ached in the back of her throat, behind her eyes.

He went on, 'What I most regret about marrying Celia is that I hurt her. But the whole experience made me wary of beautiful, socially adept women who live in cities. When you went back to Auckland I had to work out why I'd cheated you and gone behind your back, and, although I despise myself for it, I think partly it was a nasty, unconscious bit of revenge.'

The savage self-disgust in his tone chilled her. 'Is it over?' she asked.

His smile was mirthless. He lifted his hand and held it against her heart, monitoring her life force.

'It's over,' he said in a raw voice. 'I thought I loved her, but clearly I didn't. I didn't want to call what I felt for you love because it had let me down before, but if feeling that I own you, body and soul, is love, then that's what this is.

'I would die to save you from any pain. I want you to bear my children, hold my hand, live with me and be happy, be with me when I take my last breath so that your face is the last thing I see. If you believe nothing else, believe that. Can't you tell, my heart? I lose control when you are near me; I behave like a fool. I more or less kidnapped you and tried to tell myself that it was to keep you away from any developers, when really it was because I wanted you in my house.'

'You did have the first refusal waiting for me to sign,' she said teasingly.

His laughter was low and quiet and savage. 'Yes. Oh, I fought it. I told myself that it was business. I refused to believe that I had watched a woman dressed in outrageous clothes totter across a paddock and lost my heart like that, in that first minute. When that horse came towards you I had to save you—because even then I knew I was saving my own life. And you fitted in my arms as if you'd been made for them. I felt all sorts of primitive emotions—that you were my woman and that I'd fight to keep you there for the rest of our lives together.'

Jan closed her eyes. 'Yes,' she said. 'Just like that. As though I'd come home. Wholesale surrender, damn you.'

He laughed and kissed her, and the world flamed around them again, warm with promise, with hope and laughter and love...

Much later, when the sounds of traffic had almost died completely, she kissed his shoulder and asked dreamily, 'Did you really not tell me about the portrait so that you could warn dealers in case I wanted to sell it?'

His voice was deep and dry. 'No—although I did warn everyone. It sounds ridiculous now, but I kept quiet because of the legend. I knew about it, of course, and I looked at Maria's pretty, smug little face and thought with complete and utter outrage, Damn it, I'm going to control my own life! I refuse to be manipulated into some sort of quasi-mystical union by a damned portrait. I don't believe in love at first sight—or second, or even third. I suppose I thought that by refusing to acknowledge Maria I could retain some self-respect.'

She looked down at him. His eyes were clear, almost transparent, love a silver flame in their depths. She would always be able to see it there. 'Oh, I did a lot of thinking about self-respect too.'

'If you want to sell to the developers, I can live with it.' His smile was hard. 'I won't like it, but it will be a just punishment. I had no right to try and manipulate you into selling to me.' He turned his head and kissed her neck. 'I'm sorry,' he said quietly.

'It's all right. I don't want to sell to them. I couldn't bear to spoil the bay and the hills with bachs and roads. The camp will fit in—we'll get a good architect.'

'Oh, we'll get the best,' he said, his voice deep and sure. 'It never occurred to me that you'd want to keep the bay. You'd made it fairly obvious that you thought Papanui was the end of the earth.'

'I could tell what you were thinking,' she said drily.

'So you played up to it. When I saw you at your party the comparisons with Celia were so obvious—you had that charm, that ability to make everyone think that you were interested in them alone. People laugh when you're with them, they try to attract your attention. I thought, No, damn it, not again!'

His arms tightened about her. 'I fought a losing battle until we made love. It was like reaching paradise—more than I'd ever expected, more than I had the right to hope for. But I still wasn't prepared to admit that you are more important to me than anything else in this world, more necessary to me even than Papanui.

'I told myself that I wasn't cheating you, I was just using every advantage to make sure the property came to me. And claiming Maria didn't matter because we'd be married and you'd own her then too. So I crowed a little to Derek. And when you hurled my behaviour in my teeth and I realised that my dreams were smashing around my ears, I thought, It's happened again, and this time it's my fault.'

He might have come to terms with that first marriage, but it had scarred him. Jan nodded. 'And I thought you'd slept with me so I'd sell you the land. When I discovered that the portrait was yours, it made me certain you'd used me.'

'No,' he said, his voice swift and vital and fierce. 'That night was—I still can't tell you how much it meant to me.'

She could afford to be generous. 'Me too,' she said. 'I gather you don't still think this is "some sort of quasi-mystical union," that Maria has magicked into existence?'

'I don't care,' he said calmly. 'Let her have her victory. I've had a taste of life without you, and it was worse than anything I've ever imagined. Sheer hell—and compounded because I knew it was my fault entirely.'

She kissed him. 'It's all right,' she said. 'You could start making it up to me if you like. If you can.'

He laughed. 'I can.'

Some hours later she lay against his shoulder, listening to their heartbeats slow, and asked dreamily, 'How's Tina?'

'She's fine. Do you realise just how much the workshop you gave altered her life?'

'She told me,' she said. 'I felt guilty about not remembering her.'

'She said she was on the slide towards the streets when a friend talked her into going to a workshop. You talked to them, and did exercises with them on self-esteem, but apparently what really did the trick was when you did a make-over on her and four or five others. She looked at the girl in the mirror and realised that she could be someone. So she accepted Noelle's invitation.'

'And met Brett.'

His voice was cool. 'Yes.'

'Noelle told me what happened.'

His chest lifted. 'Noelle is normally the soul of discretion. You have a way of making people confide in you.'

'Are they getting back together?'

'Yes. I think Brett really does love her, and I believe him when he says he's turning over a new leaf, but Tina has decided to stay at Papanui, where her support system is. Listening to her sing your praises, learning what you'd done for her, made me realise just how important your work is, and how necessary.'

Jan yawned, feeling repletion like warm honey flow through her. 'Good,' she said sleepily. 'I was worried about her.'

'I don't want you to worry about anything ever again,' he said, and pulled her across him, his hand lax and heavy on her hip. 'Go to sleep, now. We have a wedding to plan in the morning.'

EPILOGUE

'ANET'S always looked like a goddess,' Jan said, watching her half-sister walk out of the sea, 'but I must say pregnancy suits her. She glows.'

Lucas Tremaine, turquoise eyes shielded by dark lashes, smiled with the hungry edge that was never far from his expression when he looked at his wife. Occasionally Jan remembered that he and she had squared off in opposite corners when first they'd met; she'd rushed to protect her sister from him and been routed without mercy. They'd long ago overcome that rocky start and were now good friends.

'She always glows,' he said, making room for Anet on the rug under the pohutukawa tree. A very big man, he reached up a hand to his tall wife, supporting her as she came down beside him. Seawater collected in pearls across her shoulders, and slicked her short black hair into a smooth cap.

She grinned at him and said amiably, 'I really don't need help to sit down yet.'

'I'm practising,' he told her.

They exchanged a private smile before Anet looked around, asking, 'Have Tina and Brett gone?' as she began to dry her hair.

'Yes,' Jan said. 'Liam's had too much of everything, so they decided to take him home before he threw a tantrum.'

Just in front of them Olivia stood beside a crouching Drake, her honey-blonde hair blowing freely in the slight breeze that kept them all from suffering too much from the midsummer heat. Beside her, two boys in graduated sizes earnestly discussed with their father something they'd found in the sand. Their smaller sister clutched

186

her mother's hand, taking enthusiastic part in the conversation. Simon, Olivia's half-brother, snorkelled out in the bay with a friend. At the other end of the beach Jan's mother and stepfather walked in the shade of the trees.

That week the builders had begun the foundations for the camp buildings, and, although it had taken a fair amount of organising, Jan had gathered her family to celebrate the occasion.

A slight movement caught her attention; she turned her head to see Kear come towards them from the house, the sun catching his hair and turning it to dark flames. They had been married almost six months, and Jan had never imagined that anyone could be so happy as she was.

Her hand touched the slight thickening of her midriff. In five months' time she'd be a mother too—three months behind Anet.

She said lazily, 'Tell me honestly, Anet, do you really think Maria Lannion's miniature had anything to do with all this...' She waved a hand to encompass the bay, the water, the people walking and swimming, and Kear as he came towards them.

Anet finished drying her face and shoulders and looked at her husband with laughter lighting her silvery eyes—eyes as pale as Kear's yet entirely different in quality. 'Most of the time I think it was simply coincidence that we all met our respective loves after Maria crashed into our lives, but I suppose I must be superstitious enough to believe it, otherwise why did I give the miniature to you?'

'For the same reason Olivia handed it on to you,' Jan said. She lifted her brows at Lucas, who was watching his wife with a half-smile. 'What do you think?'

He shrugged. 'Common sense tells me it's pure coincidence. You're three beautiful women and you were all of marriageable age when the miniature turned up; it was inevitable you'd meet someone.'

'But you don't really think that, do you?'

As Kear dropped lithely to the ground behind Jan, Lucas laughed. 'Do you expect me to admit anything else?'

Kear pulled Jan so that she was sitting back against his chest. She rested lightly, secure against his warm strength, and said, 'That somehow the essence of Maria Lannion's determination and happiness entered the painting her husband did of her so that her spirit was able to affect relationships some two hundred years later? Sounds ridiculous, doesn't it?'

At that moment Olivia and Drake arrived back with their family, and the subject was abandoned, but later in the evening, when the children were asleep and they were sitting out on the terrace beneath the jewelled sky, it arose again.

'And so the warning in Maria's note doesn't apply to you Lannions?' Anet asked Kear.

'The family seem to have taken the view that it was directed at anyone outside it who came into possession of the miniature,' he said. 'But she's always been a good luck charm, matrimonially speaking.'

Not for the first time, Jan thought of his first marriage, contracted when Maria was away on her travels. A slight shiver pulled her skin taut.

'I worried,' Olivia said, speaking thoughtfully, 'that the portrait might produce an unnatural desire, that it would fade when I handed on the miniature. In a way I think that was the final test; we had to pass the portrait on.'

'I,' said Drake, his deep voice calm and sure and amused, 'didn't need Maria Lannion to convince me I'd found the woman I wanted to marry. I knew within a couple of minutes of seeing you again.'

Lucas laughed lazily. 'I saw Anet rise out of the sea, and that was it for me.'

'And I saw a pretty pink mushroom totter across the grass at a polo match,' Kear said, his indolent tone not quite hiding the deep emotion beneath the words. 'Goodbye, peace. Welcome, happiness.'

It was good to laugh together in the soft darkness, good to know that whatever the reason, they were secure. If the miniature of Maria Lannion had any sort of power, it was the power of love.

ℋarlequin ℛomance ®

celebrates forty fabulous years!

Crack open the champagne and join us in celebrating Harlequin Romance's very special birthday.

Forty years of bringing you the best in romance fiction—and the best just keeps getting better!

Not only are we promising you three months of terrific books, authors and romance, but a chance to win a special hardbound 40th Anniversary collection featuring three of your favorite Harlequin Romance authors. And 150 lucky readers will receive an **autographed** collector's edition. Truly a one-of-a-kind keepsake.

Look in the back pages of any Harlequin Romance title, from April to June for more details.

Come join the party!

Look us up on-line at: http://www.romance.net

HR40THG2

MILLION DOLLAR SWEEPSTAKES
OFFICIAL RULES
NO PURCHASE NECESSARY TO ENTER

1. To enter, follow the directions published. Method of entry may vary. For eligibility, entries must be received no later than March 31, 1998. No liability is assumed for printing errors, lost, late, non-delivered or misdirected entries.

   To determine winners, the sweepstakes numbers assigned to submitted entries will be compared against a list of randomly, preselected prize winning numbers. In the event all prizes are not claimed via the return of prize winning numbers, random drawings will be held from among all other entries received to award unclaimed prizes.

2. Prize winners will be determined no later than June 30, 1998. Selection of winning numbers and random drawings are under the supervision of D. L. Blair, Inc., an independent judging organization whose decisions are final. Limit: one prize to a family or organization. No substitution will be made for any prize, except as offered. Taxes and duties on all prizes are the sole responsibility of winners. Winners will be notified by mail. Odds of winning are determined by the number of eligible entries distributed and received.

3. Sweepstakes open to residents of the U.S. (except Puerto Rico), Canada and Europe who are 18 years of age or older, except employees and immediate family members of Torstar Corp., D. L. Blair, Inc., their affiliates, subsidiaries, and all other agencies, entities, and persons connected with the use, marketing or conduct of this sweepstakes. All applicable laws and regulations apply. Sweepstakes offer void wherever prohibited by law. Any litigation within the province of Quebec respecting the conduct and awarding of a prize in this sweepstakes must be submitted to the Régie des alcools, des courses et des jeux. In order to win a prize, residents of Canada will be required to correctly answer a time-limited arithmetical skill-testing question to be administered by mail.

4. Winners of major prizes (Grand through Fourth) will be obligated to sign and return an Affidavit of Eligibility and Release of Liability within 30 days of notification. In the event of non-compliance within this time period or if a prize is returned as undeliverable, D. L. Blair, Inc. may at its sole discretion, award that prize to an alternate winner. By acceptance of their prize, winners consent to use of their names, photographs or other likeness for purposes of advertising, trade and promotion on behalf of Torstar Corp., its affiliates and subsidiaries, without further compensation unless prohibited by law. Torstar Corp. and D. L. Blair, Inc., their affiliates and subsidiaries are not responsible for errors in printing of sweepstakes and prize winning numbers. In the event a duplication of a prize winning number occurs, a random drawing will be held from among all entries received with that prize winning number to award that prize.

5. This sweepstakes is presented by Torstar Corp., its subsidiaries and affiliates in conjunction with book, merchandise and/or product offerings. The number of prizes to be awarded and their value are as follows: Grand Prize — $1,000,000 (payable at $33,333.33 a year for 30 years); First Prize — $50,000; Second Prize — $10,000; Third Prize — $5,000; 3 Fourth Prizes — $1,000 each; 10 Fifth Prizes — $250 each; 1,000 Sixth Prizes — $10 each. Values of all prizes are in U.S. currency. Prizes in each level will be presented in different creative executions, including various currencies, vehicles, merchandise and travel. Any presentation of a prize level in a currency other than U.S. currency represents an approximate equivalent to the U.S. currency prize for that level, at that time. Prize winners will have the opportunity of selecting any prize offered at that level; however, the actual non U.S. currency equivalent prize if offered and selected, shall be awarded at the exchange rate existing at 3:00 P.M. New York time on March 31, 1998. A travel prize option, if offered and selected by winner, must be completed within 12 months of selection and is subject to: traveling companion(s) completing and returning of a Release of Liability prior to travel; and hotel and flight accommodations availability. For a current list of all prize options offered within prize levels, send a self-addressed, stamped envelope (WA residents need not affix postage) to: MILLION DOLLAR SWEEPSTAKES Prize Options, P.O. Box 4456, Blair, NE 68009-4456, USA.

6. For a list of prize winners (available after July 31, 1998) send a separate, stamped, self-addressed envelope to: MILLION DOLLAR SWEEPSTAKES Winners, P.O. Box 4459, Blair, NE 68009-4459, USA.

Free Gift Offer

With a Free Gift proof-of-purchase
from any Harlequin® book, you can receive
a beautiful cubic zirconia pendant.

This stunning marquise-shaped stone is a genuine cubic
zirconia—accented by an 18" gold tone necklace.
(Approximate retail value $19.95)

Send for yours today...
compliments of  HARLEQUIN®

To receive your free gift, a cubic zirconia pendant, send us one original proof-of-purchase, photocopies not accepted, from the back of any Harlequin Romance®, Harlequin Presents®, Harlequin Temptation®, Harlequin Superromance®, Harlequin Intrigue®, Harlequin American Romance®, or Harlequin Historicals® title available in February, March or April at your favorite retail outlet, together with the Free Gift Certificate, plus a check or money order for $1.65 U.S./$2.15 CAN. (do not send cash) to cover postage and handling, payable to Harlequin Free Gift Offer. We will send you the specified gift. Allow 6 to 8 weeks for delivery. Offer good until April 30, 1997, or while quantities last. Offer valid in the U.S. and Canada only.

Free Gift Certificate

Name: _____

Address: _____

City: _____ State/Province: _____ Zip/Postal Code: _____

Mail this certificate, one proof-of-purchase and a check or money order for postage and handling to: HARLEQUIN FREE GIFT OFFER 1997. In the U.S.: 3010 Walden Avenue, P.O. Box 9071, Buffalo NY 14269-9057. In Canada: P.O. Box 604, Fort Erie, Ontario L2Z 5X3.

FREE GIFT OFFER   084-KEZ

ONE PROOF-OF-PURCHASE
To collect your fabulous FREE GIFT, a cubic zirconia pendant, you must include this original proof-of-purchase for each gift with the properly completed Free Gift Certificate.

084-KEZ